CAROLYN 3 SLOAN

THE MALL

GANGS, GHOSTS & GYPSIES

HIPPO

Hippo Books
Scholastic Publications Limited
London

Other titles in **The Mall** series:

1 Setting Up Shop
2 Open for Business
4 Money Matters

Scholastic Publications Ltd.,
10 Earlham Street, London WC2H 9RX, UK

Scholastic Inc.,
730 Broadway, New York, NY 10003, USA

Scholastic Tab Publications Ltd.,
123 Newkirk Road, Richmond Hill,
Ontario L4C 3G5, Canada

Ashton Scholastic Pty. Ltd.,
P O Box 579, Gosford, New South Wales,
Australia

Ashton Scholastic Ltd.,
165 Marua Road, Panmure, Auckland 6,
New Zealand

First published by Scholastic Publications Ltd, 1989

Text copyright © Carolyn Sloan, 1989

ISBN 0 590 76036 X

All rights reserved
Made and printed by Cox & Wyman Ltd., Reading, Berks
Typeset in Plantin by AKM Associates (UK) Ltd., Southall, London

The story so far . . .

In **Setting Up Shop**, six teenagers from different backgrounds get part-time jobs in Monk's Way, a new shopping Mall built on the site of a 16th century monastery. They settle in helping their bosses to get the shops ready for the opening day.

In **Open for Business** they find that having a job can lead to problems . . .

IAN CARTER is nearly sacked from Harmony Records by his crooked boss Hodson when his father, a flash record producer, cons Hodson into thinking pop star Aladdin Kaftan is opening Harmony exclusively.

AMANDA BURNES-PARTRIDGE and

KAREN GREEN confess they have been lying to each other, Amanda to hide her rich background with her expensive school, pony and almost-stately home. Karen claims that her father works at Burnes on the bypass, which is Amanda's father's business. In fact Mr Green is an idle scrounger; Karen has six younger brothers and she keeps her job a secret from her family. She works at Victoriana for Mrs Kendall, an antique jewellery expert who teaches her to recognize valuable fake jewellery at jumble sales. There are rumours that the Mall is haunted by monks' ghosts, but Mrs Kendall is unduly shocked to hear the ghost may be a woman . . .

Amanda gives up her job at Grozzis, the Italian restaurant where she has been overworked and harassed by Papa Grozzi and his son Antonio, and finally embarrassed by her yuppie "friends" including her snobby mother's pet, the Hon. Nigel Andringham-Gifford.

Ramu Krishna in his family's shop Bizarre! next door is upset by the Grozzis' behaviour, but Amanda is equally upset to find that Ramu's sister, Sushi, seems to be kept hidden away whilst her family arrange her marriage to a much older man.

JAKE CROSSLYN has good news – his bullying father has left home, but now he feels responsible for his mother, verging on a breakdown, and his little handicapped sister, Sophie. He is terrified of losing his two jobs in the Mall – at the toy shop and in the management office.

When Mrs Benson, the Manageress, discovers Jake has (illegally) been doing two jobs, Jake blames "Slime" Hawkins for betraying him and they fight. Jake breaks down and tells Mrs Benson about his family. She arranges help from a social worker for them, but is concerned to learn later that money and toys are missing from the toy shop.

SIMON HAWKINS is a mystery – no one knows where he came from or lived for the first twelve years of his life. Ben and Cliff, two younger boys in care with him at The Grange Children's Home have theories: Cliff, whose parents are both in prison, believes Simon is a sinister underworld figure. Ben, abandoned by his parents, is more sensitive, and believes Simon once lived in a deep forest with "Someone Very Special".

Bottling up his past makes Simon aggressive and difficult. After the fight with Jake he has a row with Chris Burrows, his boss at the antique furniture shop, Pinewood. Chris, who believes a master craftsman has taught Simon his extraordinary carpentry skills and knowledge of wood, reluctantly sacks him. Simon tries to get another job, but he is rejected by two shopkeepers.

KATHY ROBERTS sympathizes with Simon. She comes from a Salvation Army family and has tried to befriend him before. They arrange to meet. But Kathy gets stuck in the staff lift with IAN CARTER for two hours. They both work for Harmony Records at different times and have not met before, but have developed a friendship by leaving each other notes at work. Ian is painfully shy, but Kathy puts him at ease. They sing to while away the time and discover they are both musical. Ian plays piano and Kathy is a singer/guitar player.

When they are rescued from the lift they run into Simon who has been waiting for Kathy and believes she has stood him up for Ian . . .

Chapter One

"I wish I'd had a camera – it was hilarious. Like scenes from a cops-and-robbers film!"

"What was? What happened?" The regulars of the Corbury Arms were jostling for positions near the window that overlooked the Monk's Way Shopping Mall.

"I saw these two kids come out arm in arm. Couldn't have been more than thirteen or so – quaint little Darby and Joan . . . Then jealous lover came raging up like a bull and hurled himself at the boy . . . they were rolling about in the street giving each other real GBH!

"Next thing, up drives a mini with a couple of Salvation Army officers, then the cops turn up and then a bloke like a boxing promoter in a dirty great Daimler . . . They all joined in the fight and the Monk's Way security guy was hopping round them like a clockwork chicken. I tell you, it was hilarious!"

It was anything but hilarious to timid Ian. He sat in the front seat of the old Daimler harbouring enough grudges against Slime Hawkins to start an epidemic.

"You are a pillock, Ian!" said Bernie Carter as he slammed the accelerator and drove straight across a new roundabout system. "I didn't start getting into fights over girls until I was years older than you." There was a note of grudging admiration and even envy in his voice, as if he'd like to start doing it all over again.

Ian shuddered and said nothing.

"Cheer up! It's not the end of the world!" his father went on, without a shred of sympathy. "You should have been home tonight. I've got a new band doing a demo and their keyboard player's got toes for fingers. You could have taken over, been in with a chance."

"Chance of what?" Ian asked sullenly.

"Of being on their single. We're in the middle of a new rehearsal set, you still can . . ."

"I don't think I feel like it, Dad . . ."

"You can't chuck up a chance . . . You're all right, aren't you?"

"I wondered when you'd ask that," said Ian bitterly.

"Steady on . . . course you'll be a bit bruised . . ." Mr Carter stopped on the roadside and looked at his son carefully. "Sorry Ian . . . you do look a bit ropey. Bit shocked, eh?"

Ian nodded. "I feel like I've just gone six rounds with Bruno. Everything aches . . ."

"Maybe you should have an X-ray . . ."

"The police surgeon said it wasn't necessary."

"Well, we'll put something on that eye . . . and your lip."

"They did that."

"Let's see your hands – they O.K?" said Bernie Carter with such sudden concern that Ian smiled as far as his cut lip would let him.

"They're O.K. Knuckles a bit grazed. I hope it shows on Slime. Hope he's really sore . . ."

"Who's the girl?"

"Kathy. Kathy Roberts. She works for Harmony Records too. I can't think why she was going to meet Slime," Ian said miserably.

"Double-dating. We all get stood up by women some time or another. Forget this one. She sounds a right little tart."

"She's not! It's not like that, Dad. Kathy's a really nice girl. I bet she's never been on a date in her life!" said Ian furiously.

"O.K. Keep your rag. I didn't know it was serious."

"It's not like that either. I'd never met Kathy until this evening. We've been writing notes to each other at work."

"Dead romantic!"

"I should have known you'd laugh. We got stuck in the lift together – that's all that happened."

"All that happened in the lift?" Bernie Carter looked at Ian curiously and nearly hit a lorry.

"We sang to pass the time. Like shipwrecked people do on life rafts, you know."

"Got a good voice, has she?"

"Yeah," said Ian, remembering her clear tone and her expressive face in the grotty little lift. Bernie Carter's imagination had gone into overdrive as usual.

"She's a Sally Ann . . ." he said speculatively. "Now, there's an idea. Hasn't been anything like it since The Singing Nun . . . put her in a uniform, you on the piano . . . you could wear the uniform too, great duo. Really marketable. I can see it all already . . ."

"I can't," said Ian wretchedly. His father was always taking things over, putting them in commercial parcels and trying to sell them. He'd been trying to sell Ian and his piano playing since he'd been small.

"She wouldn't be allowed," he said, annoyed that he hadn't know about the Salvation Army until her parents had turned up. He didn't really know anything about her at all, except that she was special and pretty and had a wonderful voice.

"Ian! What's happened? I'll make you a cup of tea . . . Maybe you should go to bed . . ." His mother was gratifyingly sympathetic and attentive. She took him a tray of soup and scrambled eggs in bed and smothered him with iodine and

4

antiseptic. "You're going to have a beautiful black eye tomorrow. You'd better stay off school – unless you want to show it off."

"I don't mind school so much. It's going to work afterwards. Hodson'll sack me if I turn up like this. He hasn't forgiven me for the Aladdin business yet, you know? Dad fixed for Aladdin Kaftan to open half the shops at Monk's Way after he'd sold him exclusively to Harmony Records."

"I know," said his mother with feeling. She had been furious with her husband for interfering and embarrassing Ian. Heaven knows, he had enough problems with his shyness. It had taken guts to go and get a job in the Mall without having all that attention forced upon him.

"I'll ring Mr Hodson tomorrow and say you're ill. Afraid you're going to be feeling pretty rough anyway."

He couldn't sleep, not just because of the throbbing bruises and cuts, but for worrying about Kathy. He wondered what sort of trouble she'd be in – what people would say about her. The other children would gossip and call her names . . . And what about the Salvation Army? He wished he knew more about them. Would she be court-martialled or something dreadful?

Then there was Mr Hodson, his boss at Harmony Records, to worry about. He didn't like Hodson, and he thought he was a crook. He hoped the computer would find out about his dodgy accounting . . . On the other hand he didn't want to lose his job. He was just getting used to it. Starting to get on with people . . . and Kathy. How would he get to see her again?

And what about Slime Hawkins? Slime had been in fights before. He seemed to have trouble keeping out of them, vicious yob! He was scared of meeting Slime again now. Every time he closed his eyes he imagined he could hear Slime climbing up the drainpipe outside his window, coming to get him.

"Do up your seat belt, Simon." Geoffrey Bates spoke kindly enough but Slime Hawkins just stared sullenly out of the window. "Simon, I'm waiting."

"What's it matter?"

"It's the law and we're sitting outside the police station. Come on, I don't want to sit here all night. You're not the only problem I've had today."

"Oh, we're all problem kids, aren't we?" said Simon caustically. "That's why we're in care. I suppose I'm the worst."

"There isn't a league table. Belt up and we'll talk about it at home. And don't say it's not your home," he added quickly.

"It's not . . ."

"It's where you live at the moment. Now belt up before I put the ruddy thing round your neck and pull it hard."

Simon did up his belt gracelessly. "That tight

enough for you?" Mr Bates started the car and drove in silence. Simon didn't like the silence. He wished Bates would rant and rave, tear him off a strip for fighting again. The silence un-nerved him.

"What did you mean when you said it's my home 'at the moment'?" No answer.

"Go up to your room," Geoffrey Bates said when they got to The Grange.

"But . . ."

"Do as you're told. Mrs Bates'll have a look at your war wounds."

The house had gone silent, the television was turned off, the chatter and the ping-pong stopped, intrigued faces peered round doors.

"Slime's in real trouble this time," they seemed to gloat. "Let's see what's going to happen to him now!"

Simon didn't want to go to his room. He didn't want to be alone with his guilt. He wanted it all out in the open straight away. He wanted to know if he was going to stay at The Grange or if he was going to have to move on and start again somewhere else. He stopped with his hand on the banisters. "I'm sorry, Mr Bates," he muttered.

"What was that? Speak up."

"What's going to happen to me?"

"We'll have to see. If the other boy's father takes a case against you it'll be the Juvenile Court and then . . . Well, we'll see." Simon nodded and went slowly, painfully up the stairs. Geoff Bates watched him go and hoped he was doing the right thing. All Simon's prickles were showing. He was huddled deep into himself. No use trying to talk to him now – the huddle would only deepen. Bates longed to reach out after the boy, but this time, he decided, Simon would have to come to him.

Simon went to his little room under the eaves that led directly off Ben and Cliff's bigger room. Surely Bates wasn't going to leave him to stew all night. Well, if he was that was how it would be. *He* wasn't going crawling back downstairs. Mrs Bates came and looked at his injuries and sighed over them, but said nothing about the cause. It seemed like a week before Ben and Cliff came up to bed.

Simon wanted to scream out his rage, break up his room, jump out of the window and run. He curled up on his bed and stuck his balled fists in his eye sockets instead, and waited, and longed for someone to come.

Who? He'd isolated himself from everyone he knew now. He hated them all anyway, and they all hated him. Even the memory of the old man haunted him that evening. He could see his old man's face, the tired grey eyes behind their gold rimmed glasses, the rough, gnarled, gentle old man's hands, the cheeky smile. "No, no, no! Go away!" he sobbed into his pillow. "You left me too. You shouldn't have done that. Why did you go? Why? Why!"

Ben and Cliff came into their room, tiptoeing and whispering. Simon mopped his eyes with a

8

corner of his duvet and listened to them trying to be quiet. He knew they were apprehensive, uncertain of his mood. Suddenly he wanted to reassure them.

"Ben? Cliff?" he called. "What are you making so much noise for?"

"Sorry, Slime, we were trying not to disturb you," said Ben, standing in the door in his underpants. "You O.K?"

"Course I am."

Both the younger boys came in then, their curiosity overtaking their uncertainty.

"Is it true what they're saying? You put the other bloke in hospital?" Cliff was impressed. Slime was getting professional.

"No. No! I hope not."

"Why not? You should of killed him!"

"You'd have liked that, you bloodthirsty louse!"

"I could have sold my story to the papers. I LIVED WITH A RABID KILLER."

"Shut up!" said Ben uneasily. "Slime likes rabbits. Here, Slime – you hungry? You didn't have any supper."

"What's that?" asked Simon suspiciously as Ben produced a squashed and greasy envelope.

"Chicken and ham pie. You like it."

"There's no meat," said Simon, eating the crust.

"Well, I had to have something, didn't I?"

"Yes. Thanks, Ben. What did you keep for me, Cliff. The rind off your cheese?"

"We didn't have cheese," said Cliff, scowling. "You can get chips at the police station. If they keep you long enough. My Dad says they send out for a take-away for you sometimes."

"Well, I'm not a long-term criminal like your dad, am I?"

"No," said Cliff, disappointed. "They said there was a girl involved. Was it stuck-up Mandy?"

"Don't be daft. Would I be waiting for her? I can't afford the Ritz, you know. It was little Kathy, Kathy Roberts. There's someone else who'll never speak to me again."

"You were taking her out?"

"It wasn't like that," said Simon, sighing angrily. "We were just going to have a coffee after she'd got her Mum's birthday present . . . She got stuck in the lift with this other boy, Ian something, works at the record shop. I didn't know until it was too late . . . I'd waited and gone away and gone back and . . . out they came, and in I went . . . and now God knows what's going to happen next!"

"Girls!" said Cliff knowledgeably.

"Why were you going to meet Kathy?" asked Ben curiously.

"She'd been nice to me. I lost my job at Pinewood. The Burrows sacked me . . . I lost my temper. I tried to get another job. The Grozzis wouldn't have me at their restaurant because I wasn't pretty and feminine enough . . . and the Krishnas won't employ anyone at Bizarre! unless they're Indian or relatives . . . Kathy was just being sympathetic. That's why she said she'd meet me."

"That's sexist and racist!" said Cliff triumphantly. "We'll do 'em over for you, Slime!"

"Don't be stupid. Keep out of it."

"You've got to fight for your rights, Slime."

"I don't want to fight . . ."

"That's rich coming from you! You've duffed up more people in the last week than a professional hit man."

"Oh, go to bed. Violence doesn't answer anything. I know that."

Mrs Bates came on her evening round. "All right, Simon?"

"Yeah. Thanks."

"Mr Bates will talk to you in the morning. You won't be going to school. You'll be suspended for a couple of days."

"Then what?"

"We'll find out. Mr Bates has been doing quite a lot on your behalf this evening. Try and be easier to help, will you?"

"I've been thinking," said Cliff as he put his socks on inside out the next morning.

"Thinking? What with?" said Ben, who was carefully putting his socks on the right way round.

"'Bout Slime. How we're going to get his own back on the Mall for him."

"Oh yes? Us and whose army?"

"I've thought about that too. Fangs' Gang."

"Fangs' Gang?" Ben looked at him like a startled deer.

"Why not?"

"Because they're really heavy! Anyway, they wouldn't have anything to do with us Juniors. Except to get protection money with menaces. Mark Tripp got his shoulder dislocated for fifty pence."

"This is different," said Cliff confidently, "Slime's been victimized. He's been prejudiced against and provoked. Fangs' lot'll like that – they'll really go to town. Fact, they'll probably burn the whole Mall down. Well? You like to make out Slime's your mate, don't you? Now you can prove it. We'll go and see them at break."

Chapter Two

Amanda smiled to herself when she saw that the gypsies were back on a piece of common land near her home, Amberley Park. Good for them! The council had dug trenches to stop them coming the year before. They had filled the trenches with tree trunks this year, and driven their vans across them.

Smoke rose from their fires, there were interesting cooking smells coming from blackened pots and washing flapped defiantly between two vans. Comic coloured ponies, looking newly painted, were tethered to iron stakes. Children ran in and out of the vans chasing chickens and dogs. Several boys were playing football, using a complacent pony as the goalpost.

Amanda waved cheerily to them as she turned

into The Park drive. They glared at her suspiciously, and a child called out something rude. "Oh, be like that!" said Amanda, shrugging them off, but she was disappointed. She often dreamed of running wild and carefree like a gypsy, or going on the road with them as Karen Green had done. Sleeping under the stars, dawn-riding wild ponies at horse fairs . . . Karen had mentioned other things too, like being moved on and abused, like muddy sites and keys to dirty toilet blocks and being cold at night.

"Amanda? Is that you, darling?"

"No. I'm a gypsy, come to sell you clothes pegs, Missus. Cross me palm with silver and . . ."

"Amanda, that's not funny!" her mother said tetchily. "They've already been here several times wanting to tarmac the drive and cut down trees . . . I've rung the police three times."

"What for?" said Amanda, stretching out on a leather sofa next to the inglenook fireplace.

"To get them moved on, of course. Have you seen the mess?"

"It's just scrap. They have to trade in scrap – it's their living. Anyway, they're not on our land. What are the police going to do?"

"Nothing of course. Oh, they've got lots of excuses, like Brandinglea's a targeted area for a permanent site . . . I'm getting up a petition to see that they're targeted somewhere else."

"I bet Daddy won't sign it. I think it's really unfair. Gypsies are an ethnic minority. They ought to be protected."

14

"You don't know what you're talking about," said her mother dismissively. "Anyway, someone much more interesting came. Guess who! Nigel Andringham-Gifford! He rode over on his father's hunter. He's turning into such a nice young man . . ." Amanda pretended to throw up.

"Amanda!"

"Sorry, but Nigel's an absolute cretin. He's the pits, I hope he rode off again!"

"He's coming back . . ."

"Then I'll be out. He came down to Monk's Way today with a bunch of Hooray Henrys and some of the girls from my school . . . They just came for laughs. It was really embarrassing. They sent me up something rotten."

"What an expression! Two weeks working in that wretched shopping place and you're talking like a market trader. Nigel's got lovely manners, I do wish you could make friends with him."

"Nigel's got the manners of a pig. No, he hasn't – that's unfair to pigs. You should have heard that lot, ordering me about like a serving wench . . ."

"Which is precisely what you are. Do give it up now. You've made your statement."

"I gave in my notice at the Grozzis today. Happy now?"

"That's wonderful news!" Her mother was so genuinely pleased that Amanda hesitated to go on . . .

"But, uhm . . . I've got another job. It's sort of

15

the same but different. Pattie's Pantry. Still kitchen work – not so up-market as the Grozzis but better money. And they want me to do early morning shifts."

"They *what*?"

Amanda glanced at her mother's shocked face and decided she had to go on being defiant. "It's within the law. Daddy'll vouch for that. As long as we don't start before seven and don't work before school. So when the holidays start and on Saturdays . . ."

"Now you're being completely ridiculous!"

"No, I'll have to get up earlier. I'll still feed Tessa and muck her out and make my bed . . ."

"Those wretched buses you catch don't run that early. Do they?" said Mrs Burnes-Partridge icily.

"I'll go on my bike."

"Over my dead body!"

"Why, are you going to lie in the road?"

"Just stop this nonsense. I can hear a horse, it must be Nigel! Go and change, quickly . . ." Amanda tried to escape, but Nigel had ridden up to the open window and his fruity voice echoed round the room.

"Hullo again! Amanda back yet?"

"Yes I am," said Amanda, "and you can stop braying like a donkey. You've got a nerve coming here after that fiasco in Monk's Way!"

"Bit of a giggle, wasn't it?" Nigel dismounted and faced her through the window. "Well, wasn't it?"

"It might have amused your tiny mind, but it humiliated me. It got me the sack. Oh, thanks a million for coming!"

"I thought you could take a joke . . . Mans, it was just a bit of fun . . ."

"It wasn't fun to me! I worked hard to keep that job . . ."

"Come off it! Playing waitresses . . ."

"Just what I said," Mrs Burnes-Partridge edged her way into the argument. "Now this job caper is over."

"No it's not. I told you, Mummy, I'm going to work at Pattie's Pantry. But right now I'm going to see Tessa."

"Good," said Nigel, "I'll come with you!"

Amanda jumped through the window and ran towards the paddock. Nigel followed her, still braying.

"Stop being so stupid, Mans, and what's all this about not coming to my party?"

"I was. Suddenly I've got a prior engagement."

"That's a bit off. How do you think I feel?"

"If you feel slapped in the face, then good. Because that's how I want you to feel. Now shift your corpse off my manor!"

Nigel turned his horse and led it away, dispirited. He had thought he understood Amanda, thought she was a miniature of her mother. But golly, she was fierce! He had to admire her, in a way. He was angry with himself for misreading her, angry because she had made him seem stupid and arrogant, angry because he

17

really liked her and couldn't go back and say so.

Tessa was being arrogant on the far side of the paddock. She tossed her head and then went on grazing when Amanda called her. She usually did that – it was one of her tricks. But today Amanda was more annoyed than amused. Abba, the little companion donkey, came trotting up busily and nuzzled for the apple that was normally ready for her. Amanda hugged her neck. "You don't put on airs, Abba, do you? You're not horribly well bred like Tessa and Nigel . . . You're you and you're adorable. Like Karen Green. She's coming tomorrow to ride Tessa. You'll like her. She's honest and real and . . . Oh! Just wait, you'll see!"

Amanda met Karen off the bus the following afternoon.

"It's this way," she said, climbing over a wall. She didn't want to take Karen up the long drive and have her put off by the imposing grandeur of Amberley Park. Suddenly the mansion, whose stately grandeur and history she loved, was a looming embarrassment.

"Fields! Open spaces, freedom!" said Karen, loving it and sticking a grass blade in her mouth. "It's really great getting off concrete for a change. Where's your place? What's that over there? A hotel?"

"That *is* our place," Amanda said quietly. "Karen, I tried to tell you . . ."

"But it's a flaming great palace! . . . You're joking, Mandy. They do coach trips to stately homes like this from the bus station!"

"It's a house," Amanda said stoically. "Some houses are bigger than others, that's all."

"You can say that again!"

Five minutes later they had approached the back of Amberley Park. Karen hadn't seen the front, with its fluted columns and the grand entrance hall.

"The stable block's here," Amanda muttered as she led Karen towards its courtyard, flanked by a dozen outbuildings the size of council houses. Karen stared all round her uneasily. It wasn't just the size of everything, but the opulence, the sheer extravagance that made her feel she didn't fit in such surroundings.

She knew it was old and she could feel its history like a mellow glow. Yet every brick and window seemed pristine new, as if it had all been delivered and put together that morning.

"I went to Hampton Court once on a school outing," Karen said to cover her awkwardness. But when she saw Tessa arch her head out of her loose box she forgot everything else.

"Mandy, she's just . . . I don't know . . . like a Stubbs painting, like really beautiful. Why don't you put her in the fields?"

"I do usually. I brought her in to groom her specially for you. I've cleaned the tack too. It's in here." Karen followed Amanda into the tack room which had been designed for a dozen horses. There were just two saddles and bridles, with TESSA inscribed on the name plate, TESSA brushes and sponges, leg bandages and hoof oil, winter and summer rugs . . . and in a corner, more rugs and brushes and a little felt saddle marked ABBA.

"Abba?" Karen asked curiously.

"Abba's a little old seaside donkey."

"Is she?" said Karen with a sinking feeling that she was going to ride a seaside donkey behind Amanda on her beautiful pony.

"She's Tessa's friend. They're inseparable. Tessa was very highly strung when she first came. We got Abba to calm her . . ." Amanda lifted one of Tessa's gleaming saddles onto her forearm. "This one OK for you?"

"Oh . . ." said Karen, taken aback . . . "I don't know . . ."

"You haven't changed your mind, have you? She's quite safe."

"I'd rather ride bareback if that's all right. I tried a saddle once and I kept slipping off." Amanda looked at her doubtfully.

"Tessa's not used to being ridden bareback . . . but if that's what you want, fine."

Mrs Burnes-Partridge put her head round the door curiously.

"Amanda?"

"My mother," said Amanda unnecessarily.

"Hullo, Mrs Burnes. Pleased to meet you," said Karen politely, noticing at once how like Amanda she was. Attractive and stylish, she was wearing a gardening hat and gloves, designer jeans and a casual silk shirt. She lacked Amanda's open friendliness, though.

"This is Karen, the friend I told you about. She's come to ride Tessa."

Mrs Burnes-Partridge nodded and forced a little smile. She ran her eyes over the new friend and saw a neat little figure with gingery hair escaping frizzily from a Snoopy hair slide. Her clothes were neat but worn: clean faded jeans and a fresh T-shirt, pastel polka-dot socks and scrubbed trainers.

"You'll need some riding clothes. Amanda's got a spare set. Get your other jods, darling, and a hard hat . . ." Karen looked to Amanda for help.

"She's O.K. like that," said Amanda, "Don't fuss, Mum. Karen rides bareback."

"Oh. Well, I don't ride myself. I suppose you know what you're doing," said Mrs Burnes-Partridge, turning away with a condescending glance.

"Don't mind her," said Amanda, leading Tessa out and slipping the bridle up her nose. "She always thinks you have to dress up for everything."

"She's ever so glamorous, Mandy," said Karen, watching her move elegantly as she deadheaded roses. "Did she use to be a model?"

"She does stuff for charity shows sometimes," said Amanda carelessly, "Do you want to use the mount or shall I give you a leg-up?" Tessa

21

pricked up her ears with interest as Karen slipped lightly on her back. "Sure you're O.K. like that? Don't pull hard on her mouth. She . . ."

"Don't worry, we'll be fine. Where can we go?"

"Across the paddock and then anywhere you like. Watch out for rabbit holes in the long meadow by the stream . . . and don't try and jump the . . ."

Karen and Tessa had gone. They were already across the cobbled yard and cantering on the grass track down to the paddock.

"Blimey!" said Mr Mathers, coming round the corner with a pitchfork of hay. "Who's that bareback on the 'oss?"

"Friend of mine. D'you think it's all right? She hasn't got a hat. I hope she doesn't fall off . . ."

"That 'uns not like to fall off! Look at her go – that's animal meets animal, that is!"

"What do you mean, Mr Mathers?"

"Just the way . . . they look like they were made for each other. Even got the same coloured hair! I saw a film once about this wild lad and a Camargue pony . . ."

"Oh, did you?" said Amanda politely, but she was furious with him. Tessa was hers! Karen shouldn't look better on her than she did! She stalked angrily across the yard, her boots ringing on the cobbles and her tight jodhpurs making rasping noises as her legs brushed against each other.

She wanted Karen to enjoy her ride. Of course she did. She didn't have to be grateful or anything . . .

As soon as Karen got out of sight of the house and on to open grassland, she let Tessa have her head and gave way to a wild feeling of pure happiness and exhilaration. It was wonderful to be on a horse again, especially one as fit and responsive as this one. Her cramped home and the demanding horde of sticky brothers were a lifetime away. She was back at the Appleby Fair again with her gypsy cousins. She was eight again and free – even the sun shone from a perfect summer sky. Wild flowers and clear bird song, fume-free air and clean clean grass! Even the ditches were clean and smelled of honest brown-earth brackishness!

She slowed Tessa down to a walk to enjoy it all. And then there was another smell wafting through the soft afternoon. Wood smoke. She came out of a copse of birch trees and there they were – gypsies!

As she trotted Tessa towards them Karen could hear the squabbling children, the clanks and squeal of tools on metal. There was a smell of burning rubber now, and she could see the sun glinting off silver metal trailers. But that was all right, that was a part of it all too.

There was a man leading a trotting pony on the outskirts of the encampment. He saw Karen approaching and turned and leaned on the fence to watch her. His face was kippered by the wood smoke and gnarled beyond its years, but still familiar.

"Hullo!" Karen called out teasingly. The man grunted and pulled his cap down over his face. He wasn't looking at her, he was looking at Tessa. Well, he would be, wouldn't he?

Now he had let the pony go and was climbing over the fence. His eyes, still running over Tessa, blinked like adding machines.

"That's a nice bit of horse flesh you got there, my dear. Not thinkin' of selling, are you?"

"Selling?" Karen laughed delightedly. "Sorry, Uncle Arthur, she isn't mine to sell!"

The man raised his head suspiciously. He stared at Karen now and then spat and hit the fence.

"Karen. It has to be! God's honest truth. Malcolm's girl sitting on five grand's worth of horse!"

Chapter Three

Uncle Arthur approached Tessa, whistling through his teeth. He ran his hand over her flanks and down her legs. "Where did you get her?" Karen nodded in the direction of Amberley Park.

"The girl who lives there asked me over for a ride."

"Oh, them," he said contemptuously, and then turned his attention to his niece. "Well then, Karen," he said, looking at her appreciatively. "Come to see your old uncle, eh?"

"I didn't know you were here," said Karen honestly.

"Folks around?"

"No . . . they're still . . . where they were," Karen said rather shamefaced.

"Pity," grunted Uncle Arthur, "No matter, come and see your Auntie Rosa." He stamped down a section of the fence and Karen led Tessa through it. They were soon engulfed in an admiring crowd of noisy children and young men sizing up Tessa as Arthur had done.

"Karen!" Aunt Rosa came down the steps of her van and stood still, uncertain for a moment. Karen hesitated too, then she handed Tessa over to her uncle, and took a step towards her aunt. Rosa held out her arms and suddenly Karen was back, and the half-forgotten gypsy warmth and closeness settled round her shoulders like a comforting old blanket.

It lasted while she sat on the steps of the van, drinking tea, meeting the newest babies and recalling the babies who were now sturdy children. It lasted while they remembered funny, sunny times – hop-picking, digging potatoes, pulling in at horse fairs.

"And your father," said Rosa inevitably. "He's still living inside, then? He's still staying apart from us."

"There's another set of twins, two more boys, and a baby, Danny," Karen said quickly to divert her.

"That's seven of you's then," Aunt Rosa said sternly. "And your dad still fillin' in forms and getting money for you's, is he? Not shifting hisself to do an honest day's toil?"

Karen shrugged and then nodded. The sun seemed to lose its warmth. She longed to bring the family together again.

"You could come by, just to say hullo . . . couldn't you, Aunt Rosa?" she pleaded. "Dad and Uncle Arthur's still brothers . . ."

"He's out of the tribe. It's no use. The old lady wouldn't allow it." Karen stood up suddenly, looking around for the old lady's van. It was a little apart, freshly painted in its ancient patterns of rich colours and gold. How could she have forgotten the old lady? She who had always been in awe of her.

"Then she's still . . ."

"Course she is. She was born to see us all to the grave, that one. She'll be sending to see who the stranger is soon."

"I'm not a stranger. Can't I see her?"

"Best not, Karen love. We 'as to live with her wrath. She's still head of the tribe." Aunt Rosa stood up suddenly and stared out across the field. There was a hostile stirring among the men around Tessa. "Gorjio coming!"

Karen stood up and looked too. A boy of fifteen or so was riding up on a grey hunter, waving his whip and shouting. He seemed to be interested in Tessa.

"Karen? He with you? What you bring him here for. We got troubles enough with the residents around here."

"I don't know who it is. I wouldn't bring anyone . . ." She rushed towards Tessa protectively. The gypsies around her were ganging up aggressively. The boy didn't seem to notice.

"Hey! You there, you with the pony. Where did you get it?" he called accusingly.

"What's that to you?" someone called back angrily.

"I know who it belongs to. How did it get here?"

"You calling us horse thieves?"

"I'll call the police if you don't explain . . ." The men had taken a menacing step towards him. He dismounted and faced them. Idiot! thought Karen, but a brave idiot. Or maybe he didn't know Romanies like she did. She pushed her way into the throng.

"Tessa's with me. We're just going back." Uncle Arthur gave her a leg-up and she sprung lightly on to Tessa's back and they were gone, through the trampled fence and cantering over the meadow towards Amberley Park. She hoped the boy wouldn't come to any harm. She slowed down and looked back feeling guiltily that he had come to rescue Tessa . . . He soon caught up with her.

"You shouldn't have interfered like that," said Karen, taking the initiative.

"Me? I . . . That's Amanda Burnes-Partridge's pony! Who are you?"

"Friend of Mandy's. She asked me over for a ride."

"Oh, charming!" he said sarcastically, "So you rode Tessa straight to a gang of horse thieves. Some friend of Amanda's."

"I am! You watch what you're saying," said

Karen angrily. The boy still looked suspicious.

"Amanda would have saddled Tessa for you . . ."

"Oh, I sold the saddle to the gypsies. Now stop accusing me. Who are you, anyway?"

"Nigel Andringham-Gifford. My family live over there," he gestured with his whip.

"Oh, do they really?" said Karen, sending him up. "Well, I'm Karen Green and I live on the Redland Estate. It's very upmarket, our estate. I met Mandy at work, in the Monk's Way shopping Mall."

"Oh, I see, Karen. Sorry about what I said. But . . . seeing Tessa – she's a valuable beast and all that . . ."

"I know," said Karen, taken aback by his apology.

"Do you know those tinkers back there?"

"They're not tinkers. They're an old Romany family. They've got royal blood." She turned Tessa towards the Park, dismissing him. Nigel grinned after her. She was a bit of a novelty, not afraid to speak her mind. He liked that.

"Karen! Wait, I'll ride back with you!" She turned and saw him trying to turn his stubborn horse away from home.

"You'll have to catch me first," she said and urged Tessa into a gallop across the long meadow.

He did eventually, but it was a struggle even though his horse was bigger and stronger than Tessa.

"Do you always ride bareback?" he puffed as they rested the horses under a massive oak tree.

"Why not?"

"No reason. You're a brilliant rider. Honestly. You're a natural. Will you be coming here again?"

"I hope so."

"So do I. I'll give you a race any time."

"I wasn't racing then."

"Course you were! Anyway, maybe I'll see you . . . There's a party on Saturday. A friend of mine's giving it. Would you like to come?"

"No thanks . . . I mean . . . thanks, but . . . I can't."

"Why ever not?"

"I don't know you, do I?"

"My father's Lord Longman . . ."

"Whoever he is when he's washed," said Karen, laughing. "Sorry – my Dad wouldn't let me. Cheers! See you sometime." She rode into the home paddock leaving Nigel smiling after her, confident that she would change her mind. That would teach Amanda to stand him up!

"O.K. Karen?"

"Great! She's wonderful, Mandy," said Karen, jumping down and hugging Tessa's neck. "She's sweated up a bit. I'll rub her down." Abba was waiting at the gate when they took Tessa down to the paddock. She reached up to nuzzle her. "Beauty and the Beast," said Karen, watching them and chuckling.

"Don't be mean. Abba's beautiful too," laughed Amanda, "and she's nosey – look, she's asking Tessa where she's been and who she met and what you're like! Where did you go?"

"All over . . . I'll tell you later," said Karen with a wink.

"Oh? Tea's ready. Bet you're hungry. No chips or doughnuts, I'm afraid."

"I can't stay, Mandy. I've got to get back . . ."

"Do! Mummy's expecting you. I didn't mean it about the chips . . . Joke! I just get furious you can stay so slim with all the junk food you eat. There isn't a bus for half an hour . . ."

Karen went reluctantly and joined Mrs Burnes-Partridge at a table set under a big dark yew tree on the side lawn. She wished she'd gone and waited at the bus stop instead. It wasn't a proper tea. Mrs Burnes-Partridge smiled indulgently and glanced at Amanda when Karen took a handful of sandwiches. They were so thin they were almost transparent. She balanced them on a fluttery napkin on a plate that looked as if it came out of a doll's tea set, and then got her fingers stuck in the handle of her cup.

"Did you have a nice ride, Karen? I hope Amanda warned you about the gypsies."

"Sorry?"

"I've complained to the council, but . . ."

"My mother said I never should play with the gypsies in the wood," quoted Amanda, blocking her mother and looking at Karen curiously.

"Oh, those gypsies!" said Karen, reading the

31

situation and deciding not to get ruffled. "I met a boy called Nigel Addington-Gibson or something . . ."

"Nigel Andringham-Gifford?" said Mrs Burnes-Partridge faintly. "Did you speak to him?"

"Yes. He was riding a grey mare six sizes too big for him." She turned to Amanda confidingly, "What a prat! Do you know him, Mandy? He chatted me up like crazy. I'd just met him and he asked me to go to a party!"

Mrs Burnes-Partridge pursed her lips angrily. Amanda was intrigued.

"Are you going?"

"Of course not. I don't know him from Adam."

"I think there must have been a mistake," said Mrs Burnes-Partridge quietly, "Nigel's an Hon. he's the eldest son of Viscount Longman. Amanda, do help your friend with her cup."

"Thanks, Mandy," Karen said as she eased the dainty curved handle off her fingers. "I better be going now."

"So soon?"

"Yes, Mrs Burnes. Mum's going to bingo tonight. I've got to look after the little ones. I've got these six little brothers you see. Thanks for the tea."

The two girls walked arm in arm down the main drive. Karen looked back at the house and shook her head. "It's like . . . something out of Jane Eyre . . . No! Mansfield Park!"

"Do you read that stuff, Karen?"

"Yes, love it. I'm a born again romantic. I went straight to the Brontës from comics. A house like that should be full of rich dandies and fluttery young girls waiting to get married . . . looking out of the window . . . hearing horses' hooves on the drive . . . Are there really just the three of you here?"

"Yes. We don't have much family."

"You should come to tea at our house. We've got family all right – they swarm all over the place. They drive me mad sometimes but I like big families . . . I wish ours would get together again." She stopped and looked out over the fields reflectively.

"What do you mean, Karen? You mean your Romany family? You didn't . . . did you . . . talk to those gypsies?"

"Your mother doesn't like gypsies. She didn't like me much either."

"Oh, don't mind her. She's a bit of a snob – well, a lot of a snob but she's well-meaning really. You must come again, Karen. You won't be put off by her, will you?"

Karen walked on in silence. Amanda felt rebuffed. She wanted to hold on to Karen's friendship. Gypsies seemed to be a dodgy subject. O.K. Change it.

"Still friends? What did you say to Nigel? He is a wimp, isn't he? Are you really not going to his party?"

"God, no! My mother wouldn't like it," said

33

Karen, nudging Amanda and giggling.

"My mother would," said Amanda grimly, and then joined Karen in her giggles.

Chapter Four

"Karen? That you? Where've you been all day?"

"I told you. Riding at this girl's place."

"All day?"

"No. I went to w . . . the youth club this morning. . ."

"All right for some. Honest, love, these kids, they've been round my neck all day. Now I'm late and Elsie's picking me up. . ."

"They been fed?"

"Course they have. They'd starve if they waited for you."

"Whose kids are they? Mum? I said . . ."

"Oh, all right. Your Dad's been hollering for you."

"What for?"

"Go down the offy for his beer."

"He's got feet on the end of his legs."

"Don't think I haven't told him! Take my curlers out, there's a love, Karen. Don't you go down the offy. Let him. Stand up for yourself."

"Yeah, I think I will. Take your own curlers out, Mum!"

"You little . . ."

"Little what? I'm babysitting tonight, aren't I?"

"That's true. So you're a little saint. You're a good girl really."

"I'm still not doing your hair. I want to talk to Dad."

"Try grunting. That's what he understands best."

"There y'are," grunted her father.

"Can I turn the telly off? You're not watching it. It's about time-share villas in Turkey."

"Is it? See if there's any snooker on."

"There isn't," said Karen, turning the set off. "Do you want to know where I've been all day?"

"Yes. Where have you been? Behaving, I hope. Blimey, what's that smell?"

"What smell?"

"Dunno," he said, sniffing. "Horse muck, isn't it? Where *have* you been?"

"I went to ride my friend's pony. Dad, she lives in a mansion. I mean, really! Stable block the size of this estate. . . and I had tea with Lady Snooty on the lawn and got asked to a party by a duke's son!"

36

"Pull the other one, Karen! Dukes don't smell of horse muck," he sniffed again, puzzled, "or smoke. . ."

"I met Uncle Arthur and Auntie Rosa," Karen said, facing him defiantly.

"You what? Where?"

"They've pulled on to some common land near where this girl lives."

"You talked to them?"

"Dad, I was riding a thoroughbred at the time. They talked to me!" Her father gave an understanding chuckle. Then his face hardened.

"What did you talk about, 'part from the price of horses?"

"Things . . . good old days on the road . . ."

"They weren't all good. They're still travelling, then? Old lady still there?"

"Yes. They wouldn't let me see her. I wanted to. They treated me like . . . like an outcast. Dad, the old lady can't go on forever. You can still make up. . ."

"No!" Her father stood over her, glowering. "You had no business going looking for them."

"Why not? They're my family too! I haven't done anything, nothing at all, but I can't even visit my own grandmother!"

"You think I can? When she casts someone out they stay cast out. It's her tribe. She won't have me back."

"She would if . . ."

"You don't know what you're talking about. You're your mother's daughter. You've got

Fairground in you. Those folks aren't so parti-
cular. They don't have our pride. I'm still a
Romany. I can still step dance, still know some of
the language. Just because I married your
mother, live in a house. . . Just because I got an
independent streak . . . Karen?"

She had turned away from him with a gesture
of pent-up fury.

"Karen! Don't you turn away from me. I'm
warning you, watch it!"

"You've lost your Romany pride. That's the
truth. It's not Mum, they accepted her. Or the
house, they don't mind that even. It's the
scrounging, it's getting welfare like tinkers
or . . . or Stonehenge hippies. . ."

"Shut your mouth!" His rage was a growing,
dangerous thing and Karen knew she had gone
too far. He was loosening his belt. "I never had
cause to hit you before, our Karen," he said, his
eyes locked on hers. "But we know how to treat
our women – I haven't forgotten that . . ."

"They've got to be in the wrong first. I'm just
telling you the truth," Karen brazened. "The
women have to be proud of their men. *She* taught
me that!"

"Truth! I'll teach you *truth*!"

Karen dragged her eyes away from his glare.
She was frightened now. Three faces were
peering anxiously round the door. The big twins
and Jimmy.

"Dad? Karen? What are you doing?" asked
Jimmy nervously.

38

"It's all right, Jimmy. Don't be scared."

"Why's Dad got his belt off?"

"I haven't," Mr Green said gruffly, fumbling with the buckle.

"You going to hit Karen? Can we watch?"

"Shut up, you horrors!"

"You were the ones making the noise."

"Shut up!" He sat down heavily on the sofa. "Take them away, Karen. Go on."

Karen went to herd them up. "Move it. Up to bed."

"It's not dark yet. What's the troof you were shouting about? Can we have some crisps? Is the troof one of your monsters you made up? Is it, Karen?"

Karen got her brothers into bed and got them out again to clean their teeth. "Now go to sleep."

"I can't. I'm scared," said Jimmy. "Was Dad really going to hit you?"

"No. No, he wouldn't do that."

"Stay up here anyway. Tell us about the troof."

"Oh, all right," said Karen, shifting him over in his bunk and getting comfortable next to him.

"Once upon a time, a Troof lived in a big cave under a hill. He had long ears like a donkey and a funny red nose and green wings . . ."

"Why? Why did he have green wings?"

"Shut up. I don't know yet. The Troof was really a very good monster, but he had been sent away by the other Troofs in the valley because. . . because. . . he made too many toffee apples . . ."

The boys soon fell asleep. Karen went to her own room and found an old exercise book. She started the story again... "The Troof lived in a cave under a hill . . .

". . . he went sadly back into his cave and ate the last toffee apple. He was the Very Last of the Tribe of Troof. No one has ever seen one since." Karen put her pen down on the table with a smile and looked around the shopping centre. Papa Grozzi was hovering by her table.

"You want something else?"

"Not yet, thanks. I'm waiting for some people to show up." Papa took away her plate and glass.

"You sitta round one, two hours? Two doughnuts and a milk shake. You sit there scribblesing like this is Paris bistro? What sorta business this is for me, huh?"

"Oh, go on, Papa. I've just been here ten minutes. The others'll be here soon. We'll make the place look busy – you know we do!"

"O.K. Karen. You stay," he said, knowing that she was right. They were a lively bunch – the Monks' Way Mafia he called them. He gave her a free doughnut. "You eat, get more fat," he said reprovingly.

Ian Carter was hovering nervously. Karen smiled at him. "You're from the record shop, aren't you? Have you got that Sparky record I ordered yet for my kid brothers?"

"I don't know. I haven't been there recently. Can I sit down?"

"Sure. They're all late today. What have you done to your eye?"

"I . . . er . . . I had . . . had . . ." Ian stammered with shyness.

"Oh, hang on . . . I know. You were the one. . . Slime, the lift business . . . Sorry about that."

"It's O.K. Everyone seems to know. Is he here? Have you seen him?" Ian glanced over his shoulder timidly.

"Oh, Slime's banned from everywhere. He won't be coming."

"It wouldn't stop *him*. He doesn't listen to anyone." Ian wanted to ask about Kathy but he felt too embarrassed. "Funny place to do your homework," he said, pointing at her open exercise book. Kathy shut it quickly.

"I wasn't . . . that's just a story I was writing."

"What's it about?"

"Oh, monsters and things, for kids. I wish I could draw then I could illustrate it."

"My sister draws monsters. She does it all the time. She's really ghoulish. She does record covers for my Dad. She'd do some for you if you wanted."

"Would she? Her being a professional? Could you ask her?" Ian was about to answer when Antonio, the Grozzis' son, clapped his hand on his shoulder.

"Heh! Casanova! Got a new girl today, eh?"

Ian cringed and tried to wriggle away. He knew he was starting to blush. "Every day a new girl, ha? You're not safe with him, Karen. You

41

hear about his romance in the lift? He still got the black eye."

"Leave off, Antonio," said Karen, seeing Ian's discomfort. "Everyone knows about you and Paula-Jo in the security office."

"What do you mean?" Antonio said, pulling up a chair and lighting a cigarette arrogantly.

"Eric Bright saw you!"

"Eric Bright sees lots of things. Things that aren't there. Like ghosts in the night, and other things."

"What ghosts?" asked Jake, who had just turned up and was studying the menu critically.

"Ghosts of the monks. They come out of their graves at night and go window-shopping," said Antonio, knowing he had safely got off the subject of himself and Paula-Jo.

"I had a funny feeling one night," said Jake mysteriously. "When I was working for Mrs Benson after hours . . . Everyone else had gone home. I was walking down the main Mall and I felt there was someone beside me."

"Were you scared?"

"No. It was like . . . just having company, except there wasn't anyone there. But the thing that wasn't there was quite friendly. Antonio, can I have a Strawberry Special with a chocolate flake and a hot blackcurrant drink? You want a doughnut, Karen? Ian? I'm rich today – just been double paid."

Antonio took their orders and went off grumbling about being overworked.

"Still doing two jobs, Jake?" asked Karen.

"No. I'm sort of . . . resting at the moment. My mum's ill."

"Oh, sorry. She want any shopping or anything?"

"I can manage, thanks. This ghost . . . well, this feeling . . . it was near where you work, Karen. Antonio thinks it's funny but it isn't."

"I know it's not," said Karen. "We've got a cold patch at the back of Victoriana. My boss Mrs Kendall says that happens when you've got . . . when there's an uneasy spirit about."

"There were uneasy spirits about when they were building this place," said Jake with a shiver. "A lot of things went wrong with the building. I mean dangerous things. People nearly got killed. It was all hushed up by Mr Herb. You know? The guy who put up a lot of money at the last minute?"

"Him? I read he was tied up in that bribery and corruption thing with the council. He hasn't even been back to set up his shops. They're still boarded up," said Ian.

"I reckon he's holed up with all those criminals in Spain," said Jake knowingly. "Anyway, he didn't want the ghost story to get out in case it was bad for business."

"It'd be good," said Karen. "People love ghoulish things. Except . . ."

"What?"

"Well . . . Mrs Kendall writes stuff for the local history magazine . . . We were talking about the ghost and she was jokey about it until . . . Until I said I'd heard it was a woman, not a monk. She went all funny then and didn't want to talk about it."

"The Anchoress!" said Jake suddenly. "One of my bosses is psychic. She was talking about an Anchoress . . ."

"What's that?" asked Ian.

"A sort of nun, hundreds of years ago. She had herself bricked up in the wall – and stayed there till she died."

"Why?"

"I dunno. It's eerie though, isn't it? I don't like it."

They all looked at each other doubtfully.

"We could find out," said Karen. "We could go to the local studies place at the library. . .and to the museum. Shall we?"

"Yes . . . We could say we were doing a local history project." Ian thought for a moment. "You don't think . . . we might find out more than we want to know, do you?"

Chapter Five

Jake looked at his watch anxiously and got up to go.

"Here," said Antonio. "Don't forget your bag!" He picked up a carrier bag that jingled and tinkled musically. "What you got in there?" Antonio asked. "You rob the toy shop or something?" Jake grabbed the bag angrily and it played another tune.

"I've been buying things for my sister. What's it got to do with you?" Antonio shrugged and watched him go.

"What did I say?" he asked with mock concern.

"It's just Jake," said Karen. "He's moody these days. Worried about his mother and losing his jobs . . . Hey, Ian! That's your girlfriend, isn't it? Your Companion of the Lift!"

Ian wanted to dive into his coffee cup and pull the dregs over him. Panic rose. He wanted to meet Kathy again, desperately. But not now, not with all the curious, teasing eyes on him.

"Hullo," said Kathy, plonking her bag on a chair. "Hullo, Ian," she said separately. Karen got up to leave and gave Antonio a "shut up and leave them alone" look. He started to clear the table.

"Ian, are you all right? You've still got awful bruises . . . Did you get into trouble at home?"

"No. It helped having the bruises – Mum was really nice and Dad soon forgot about it. What about your parents?"

"They were fine, once I'd explained everything. You know I was only going to meet Slime as an Agony Aunt? Do you? He was upset about losing his job . . . he just wanted someone to talk to."

"It's O.K., really Kathy. It was just a big misunderstanding."

"Then you won't be taking a case against him?"

"No – never even thought of it. Mind, he should get punished in some way – he's always duffing people up."

"I know, but . . . well, I'm not defending him, but trouble seems to look for him. I think he's had a sad life and he can't trust anyone now. So his aggression's really a sort of fear."

"Sounds like you're defending him to me," said Ian suspiciously. "Sounds very like it. Have you seen him since. . ."

"No, I haven't," she said with a smile. "I'm still angry with him for hurting you."

"Are you?" said Ian, pleased. "Do you want a coffee or anything?"

"No thanks. I've got to go. I popped into Harmony to see if you'd been back."

"I'll go next week, when I look more presentable. Kathy . . . I . . . I was going to ring you but . . . I didn't know . . . your mum might have been angry . . ."

"Well, now you know she's not. In fact when I told her about you she said she thought you sounded really nice. She said, 'Why don't you ask him round to tea?' So I am. Will you come? Any day?"

"Thanks, I'd like to meet your mother. Specially if she's anything like you!"

"Ian!"

"What time's your young man coming, Kathy?" Mrs Roberts put her head round the kitchen door and blinked several times. "What's going on in here?"

"I've been doing some cooking," said Kathy calmly.

"You? Gracious! What are these?"

"Scones," said Kathy indignantly. "Can't you recognize them? They came out a bit flat . . . there's a cake in the oven and I bought a swiss roll and some biscuits in case the home bake went wrong. I got some sliced bread out of the freezer for sandwiches and . . ."

"That's enough! I think Prince Charming will be very impressed. He's got to be rather special to get you cooking!"

"Mum, don't say things like that when he comes, will you? Ian's really shy. He wouldn't be able to eat anything."

"I shall be the soul of discretion, Kath. Promise."

Kathy saw Ian hovering beyond the hedge. She felt a wave of affection for him. Poor Ian! Meeting people was really nerve-wracking for him."

"Hi, Ian! Come in."

He hesitated. "Your parents . . . I've never met . . . do I have to salute them?"

"No," she said with a light laugh. "They're just ordinary. Come on in, Dad's not home yet."

"Do they wear uniforms all the time?"

"No, Ian . . . Mum's a primary school teacher. Just come and meet her! You'll see."

Ian ate a lot to avoid having to talk, even though he felt half sick with nerves. It wasn't until they got on to the subject of music that he began to loosen up.

"Is that your guitar?" he asked Kathy when they had finished tea. "Will you play something for me?"

"What would you like?" she asked as she tuned it.

"Anything."

"I'll play you a couple of our new hymns," she said brightly. Ian felt uneasy. What was he doing in this quaintly old fashioned house, surrounded by Salvation Army banners and missionary photographs with a girl about to sing hymns to him? Would he end up banging a tambourine? Would they try to convert him, and wouldn't it be embarrassing if they did!

He was happily surprised when Kathy launched into a vibrant gospel number and followed it up with a spirited rock 'n' roll song. She grinned mischievously at his relief, and he lifted the lid of the piano and joined in the refrain.

An hour later they were still singing and playing. Kathy's father came in and stood quietly listening to them before they realized he was there.

"That was marvellous!" he said sincerely. Kathy's mother came in, smiling.

"I've been listening to them from the next room," she said, "It was a real treat! How did you learn to play like that, Ian?"

Suddenly Ian forgot his shyness and he was telling the family about himself as a child. How he'd toured the country with his mother when she was the Dance Captain of "Wild Fever", who'd appeared in cabaret and pantomine, television, variety shows. The piano player had befriended the three-year-old Ian and started teaching him to play before his fingers could even span three notes. He told them how he spent his wages on classical piano lessons from that same pianist, Arnold Hurst.

"Do you ever play in public, Ian?"

"Not if I can help it . . . I have to sometimes when I play for one of my Dad's bands. I get nervous and my fingers seem to stick between the notes. I wish it didn't happen," he said wistfully.

"Kathy used to be nervous, didn't you, love? But she got over it and now she's a star at the Eventide Home."

"Mum, I'm not . . ."

"What's the Eventide Home?" asked Ian.

"It's an old people's home. I go and sing for them sometimes. They're not a very demanding audience!"

"What about Beatle-Granny?"

"Oh, yes. She's a bit demanding! She knows all the Beatles' songs and she sings along with them, thumping the rhythm on her wheelchair."

"It sounds fun."

"It is. I have to do my Shirley Bassey impression for one old man."

"Maybe Ian would like to come along and play for you?" suggested Mrs Roberts.

"Oh, Mum!" said Kathy, embarrassed.

"I'd like to. I really would. What's this?" he asked, picking up some sheets of music manuscript and playing the spidery notes.

"Waterfall . . . rain . . . river . . . This is good expressive stuff."

"Don't . . ."

"Why? I like it. Elephants dum-dum-dum. Thunder boom boom boom . . .Did you write this, Kathy?"

"Yes. It's for the children at the handicapped centre. They love music. I play there too."

"Really? That's funny. Arnold, my piano teacher, he writes this sort of music. Music Therapy he calls it. He does it for mentally handicapped adults and he says it really gets through to them. Even people who've been treated like cabbages for years. . ."

"It's true, Ian!" said Kathy fervently. "It's just wonderful to see these children. Their faces light up as if . . . as if someone had reached right into their loneliness . . ." she broke off, embarrassed that she had got so emotional.

"It must be," said Ian. He started playing some of her music.

"It's good! You could put a drum machine on this . . . It would bring out the beat. And you could get some terrific effects with a synthesizer. Wait a minute . . ." Ian was suddenly engrossed in the music. Kathy and her parents swopped puzzled glances. He had forgotten they were there. "Tum-tum-*tum*-te-tum, pause, two, three, ta-ta-ta-*tum*. Have you got a pencil, Kathy? We could repeat that with the emphasis changing . . . *ta*-ta-tum-te-tum . . . Yes, then I could mix it and put it on tape with a voice-over . . ." he stopped suddenly and looked at their blank faces. "Cripes, I'm sorry! I got carried away . . . Honestly . . . it's yours. I didn't mean . . ."

"No, go on," said Kathy, "You seem to have good ideas – if I knew what you were talking about. You mean you can do all those things . . ."

"We've got a full recording studio at home."

"So you could really make something out of it all?"

"*We* could – if you wanted to. Arnold's always saying people don't use music enough. You don't think I'm being interfering . . .do you?"

"Yes – and it's great! Go on, tell me more!"

Chapter Six

"That adding-up machine's probably got it wrong," said Daph Chandler, trying to be practical.

"Jake says it can't be wrong," snapped her sister Esther. "I just wish he was here now. He could sort all this out."

"He's hardly an accountant, is he? That's what we need."

"Don't be ridiculous, Esther. We must be able to do our own accounts. Check those till roll totals again."

It was late and they were tired. They looked at each other and sighed in unison.

"Let's stop pretending. We both know there's forty pounds in cash missing. All the cheques and credit cards add up . . ."

"I knew that ages ago," said Daph miserably. "We lost twenty quids' worth of toys about the same time. It happened when . . . well, you know when."

"Jake," said Esther. "It has to be, doesn't it? I don't want to believe it, I've tried not to . . . Poor kid, he's no crook, he's a good lad. But he was desperate. Money for his mum, toys for his little sister . . . What are we going to do?"

"We ought to tell Mrs Benson."

"Oh, Daph! Don't you think the poor lad's got enough to worry about at the moment? Couldn't we wait . . ."

"Mum? Where are you?" Jake staggered in with the shopping, apprehensive as he always was these days, leaving his mother. There was a stranger sitting in his father's chair with a notebook and a spread of papers on the table in front of her.

"This is Jake," his mother said listlessly, "This is. . .sorry. I've forgotten. . ."

"Belinda," the stranger said. "Hullo, Jake."

"Hullo," said Jake, looking round the room. "Where's Sophie?" he said with sudden alarm. "Where is she? What's happening?"

"She's upstairs."

"Upstairs? Why?"

"Because she is," his mother said, frowning at him. "Belinda's a social worker. She says she's going to help us. I don't understand how but . . . Jake? Where are you going?"

"To see Sophie," he said, going up worriedly.

"Don't bring her down . . . Sorry," she said, turning to Belinda. "Jake fusses about her so . . ."

"Does he?" she said thoughtfully and turned back to her papers. "Well, that's sorted out. You'll have to take these forms to the DHSS. You understand what you're entitled to claim for the little girl now? What clinic does she go to?"

"Clinic? She saw the doctor a year or so ago . . ."

"And what did she say? Did she refer you to anyone else?"

"Yes – there was an appointment at . . . I forget where. My husband didn't . . . she didn't go, he said there was no point . . . he won't like me talking to you like this . . ."

"He's not here now, Mrs Crosslyn. You need some help and specialist advice. Can I see Sophie now?"

"He wouldn't like it," said Mrs Crosslyn fearfully.

"Do you take her out at all, Mrs Crosslyn?"

"No. No, it's not easy . . ."

"Do you mean your husband didn't like people seeing her? Is that it?"

"She's all right," said Mrs Crosslyn tearfully.

"Well, I'll pop up and see her," said Belinda, getting up determinedly. "Jake? Where are you?" A door closed and locked at the top of the stairs. She knocked on it. "Let me in, Jake. I'd like to meet your sister."

"She's not used to strangers," Jake's voice came through the door.

"I won't frighten her. Will you open the door for me?"

"You're going to take her away," said Jake aggressively.

"What are you doing?"

"I'm changing her dress. She's got a nice new dress." Belinda sat on the top stair. "O.K. I'll wait."

"I'm still waiting," she said five minutes later. "Open the door now."

"No!"

Belinda was worried. Something strange was going on. She knew she had to see the little girl. Why were they trying to stop her? What had they done to her?

"Suspended from school, lost my job – what am I supposed to do?" Simon Hawkins muttered. "It's like being public enemy number one. Like I've got something contagious."

"And none of it's your fault, of course," said Geoff Bates, who was losing his patience with Simon constantly blocking every line of communication.

"Most things aren't my fault, but there's no point in telling anyone."

"But you don't tell anyone. If you could try and explain. Let's go back to the Burrows. Now, when . . ."

"It's no good," said Simon, blocking him

again. "Other people make decisions for me these days. It doesn't matter what I say. So, do I get chucked out of here?"

"You've gone beyond what I choose for you. We'll have to wait for your reports and see if you have to come up before the Juvenile Court. I'll support you as much as I can. You know that, I hope. Just try and co-operate, will you? Meanwhile. . ."

"Oh, I get a meanwhile, do I?"

"Meanwhile you stay here. You can work in the grounds. There's plenty to do since the storm last month. You like working with trees, don't you? Well, you can lop the branches from the fallen trees and then you can have a go at putting the shed on an even keel."

"I'll need my tools."

"I'll give you a saw . . ."

"Not an axe, though. I might go and hack up some old lady."

"Simon, just stop feeling sorry for yourself or you'll lose any sympathy I've got left for you." They went down to the shed, and Geoff Bates took a saw down from the rafters.

"It's rusty. Have you got some sandpaper and some oil?"

"Yes."

"O.K."

"There's a chopper. Use that, it's sharp."

"Thanks." Simon took it and balanced it in his hands. "It's quite a good one. Not as useful as an axe . . .Thanks, Mr Bates. I'll do a good job. I suppose you want me to stay where you can see me from the house?"

"No. I trust you to stay within the grounds. See you at lunchtime."

"Why can't Slime do his own dirty work?" said Ben nervously. "I'm scared of Fangs' Gang."

"You would be," sneered Cliff, "You don't know nothing about gang warfare, do you? Slime can't come to school. He's got to stay in the grounds. Anyway, he'd probably tell us to keep away from Fangs."

"Good. Well, let's do that."

"We're his mates, aren't we? Least, I *thought* you were one as well."

"Course I am," said Ben, wishing he wasn't.

They had to get an appointment to see Fangs.

"What you want wiv 'im?"

"It's about our mate, Slime Hawkins," said Cliff. "He's been unfairly dismissed from his job in the shopping Mall and discriminalated against by the Indian shop and the Italian restaurant. We want things put right."

"Slime Hawkins? That the one been suspended from school?"

"Yes."

"Fangs'd be interested in 'im. Got a bit of previous. Sort of class Fangs might like. Lunch break in the old bike sheds. Be there."

Fangs was interested. Slime sounded like a hell-raiser after his own heart. And he'd proved he could put the boot in when it mattered. He envied Slime his mysterious past too. Fangs had a conventional family – dead boring, he called them – who had no idea that he was the leader of the school gang, or got such a kick out of frightening people. Even some of the staff were afraid of Fangs.

His gang certainly was. He had false teeth. He took them out when anyone annoyed him and handed them to one of his deputies to hold. You knew you were in for trouble when Fangs took his teeth out. He sucked his mouth in round his gums and looked horrible. Whoever held his teeth felt big and privileged. Some of the new members hung around hoping they'd get to hold Fangs' teeth for him.

"You two," he said, looking mean. "You're in care with Slime. Which one of you's Cliff?"

"Me."

"Your parents are both inside, right?"

"Yes," said Cliff proudly. "My Mum's doing five years. . ."

"Your Dad just got done for receiving though."

Ben looked anxiously at Cliff. How did he know everything about them?

"And you're Ben," Fangs turned and looked at him as if he'd accumulated in the fuzz at the bottom of a jam jar. "You're one of the little abandoned wretches. Not surprised, looking at you." Ben swallowed uncomfortably. "Well, don't snivel about it. What's the story?"

Cliff told it, exaggerating Simon's trail of bad luck until it sounded as though every shopkeeper in Monk's Way had ganged up to victimize him.

"That's enough," said Fangs, relishing the idea of the violence and vandalising to come. "We'll turn the place over. Take them away." Cliff and Ben were taken out of the bike shed roughly by two of Fangs' henchmen and pushed against a wall.

"All right, how much money have you got? Well? Go through their pockets."

"Why?" said Cliff.

"They've got less than a pound between them," said the boy who searched them sneeringly, "What d'you expect from The Grange?"

"Well, they'll have to find some money."

"What for?" asked Ben nervously.

"For insurance purposes. In case anything goes wrong, anyone gets badly hurt . . . You wouldn't want to take all the blame, would you?"

"But Fangs never said anything about paying . . ." protested Cliff.

"Fangs doesn't deal with the financial side of the business. Fangs's got other things to think about."

"How much money?" Cliff said, backing away.

"We'll start with fifteen . . . that's three five notes each if you've done your three times yet."

"Each?"

"Just for starters. You came to us. We didn't come to you. You can't back out now. We've got

60

kids in the second year paying fifteen a week. You'll find it. You'll have to. Or your matron's going to be practising a lot of first aid. She'd better be good at it too."

"Cliff . . ." said Ben on the way home after school, "Where are we going to get that sort of money?"

"We'll have to start fund-raising," said Cliff, kicking a stone viciously. "I've been asking around, what the others do. They nick stuff."

"What sort of stuff?"

"Money's best. One of our year nicked forty quid out of the toy shop till at the Mall this week. Cash is best. Shifting nicked stuff is dodgy."

"I can't do that."

"You don't have the choice. There've been a lot of football injuries this term, you noticed? I don't fancy having a football accident. Nor breaking my fingers in a locker accident . . ."

"We better ask Slime . . ."

"How can we ask Slime? We're doing it for him, aren't we? We can't get him into no more trouble." Cliff paused and sighed heavily. "Shame my Mum's inside. She'd know . . . Suppose video recorders would be best . . . if we knew where to offload them," he said professionally.

"You're just talking big, Cliff. Aren't you? Well?" Cliff didn't answer. "Thought you were. You're just as scared as I am."

"Not."

"Are."

"Oh, all right, I am. Nearly," said Cliff. "But it doesn't matter how scared we are now, does it? We're fixed." He grinned at Ben's frightened little face. "Look on the bright side, Ben. Fangs has got to leave school sometime and start a career as a big-time crook. We'll be the ones that take over!"

"I'm not having all my teeth out."

"Cut off your hand and have a hook then. That'd be really evil."

Simon cleared a path through the trees to the boundary of The Grange. He liked being alone, with the smell of fresh sawdust in the air, his hands sticky with sap. He chopped and sawed until he was stiff and sweat-stained. It was great, being amongst trees again, with just the sound of his own labours. He climbed up a willow tree to have a rest and just enjoy the trees. It wasn't a forest, not like the one he'd known. Not even a wood, just a collection of trees . . . The cleft in the willow was wide and solid. A good place for a tree house, he thought suddenly. The little kids would like a tree house. Not a twee Wendy house with windows and curtains – a rustic cabin.

He shinned down the tree. There was an old potting shed in the grounds that hadn't been used for years. Simon kicked it. The lower planks were soggy with damp rot. He sounded the upper planks – they were good, the roof beam was solid. Enough wood there . . .

He went and had a snack lunch in the kitchen with the Bateses. It was strange being the only boy in the house. The Bateses seemed different, more relaxed and jokey than usual. Simon felt relaxed too, as he told them what he had been doing. He wondered if that was what it was like having parents. He got up to go back to work.

"You know that old shed, Mr Bates? Can I knock it down? The base is rotten but there's some good timber still. It could be used for something else . . ."

"I suppose so – yes, all right Simon. But be careful, won't you." Simon ran off. Mrs Bates looked questioningly at her husband.

"Is that wise? He might hurt himself."

"He won't. I've watched him out there. He knows what he's doing. He's made a sawing block to cut up the logs. Remember those old-fashioned sawing blocks you used to see around? He's a good lad, Ruth, deep in there, he really is . . ."

"They all are," Mrs Bates answered thought-fully, but she understood what he meant particularly about Simon Hawkins.

Chapter Seven

Cliff and Ben went down to Monk's Way after school the following day.

"We could try conning old ladies," said Cliff professionally, "or nicking car radios . . ."

"Us?" said Ben scathingly. "Undo a car radio? We can't even change the battery in your alarm clock. And I like old ladies."

"You would, wouldn't you? We can't afford to be soppy about old ladies. But we'll try a bit of straightforward shoplifting first. Get a few CD's from the record shop – they're easy to sell."

Mr Hodson soon spotted them in Harmony Records.

"You two boys buying something?"

"Just looking," said Cliff. "See what we're

going to spend our pocket money on this week."

"Come back when you've got it," Mr Hodson snapped. "Go on – scarper."

They shuffled out muttering rude things about customer relations. They were moved out of several other shops.

"Suspicious lot," said Ben. "We look like robbers or something?"

"You do," said Cliff, "it's that casual saunter. You gotta go straight for something like you wanted to buy it."

"We need cash. Why don't we try the market? They keep wads of notes in boxes there."

"Market traders are sharper than this lot," said Cliff, as they peered in the window of Pampered Pets. "Look, Ben – that collecting net shaped like a cat . . . It's only held on with a couple of drawing pins . . ."

"It's the Cat Rescue League. We can't steal from cats."

"Cats won't miss it. Listen, it's a charity. Who needs charity most right now?"

"We do, but we're not cats . . ."

"Don't be wet! Go and ask for something they haven't got and I'll nick it," said Cliff, shoving Ben towards the door.

"How do I know what they haven't got?" protested Ben as they sauntered past some fish tanks. The assistant was already eyeing them suspiciously.

"Can I help you?" she asked. Cliff nudged Ben.

"We want some . . . dog biscuits," said Ben quickly as Cliff positioned himself by the counter.

"What sort?"

"Small ones."

"Small? For a puppy?"

"Yes. Yes, a puppy. A very small puppy." The assistant reached for a packet of puppy meal, keeping one eye on Cliff as he casually examined the charity bag.

"Forty pence," she said, still looking at Cliff. "You interested in cat rescue?"

"Yes," said Cliff. "Very. They need collecting for, don't they?"

"Good. Well, you can put something in for them, can't you?"

The two boys sat glumly on the wall by the fountain.

"You really are the biggest prat, asking for dog biscuits. Course they'd have dog biscuits. Why couldn't you ask for crocodile cornflakes? Something original? What are we going to do with dog biscuits – eat them?"

"No, they're disgusting," said Ben, examining the packet seriously.

"You realize we're sixty pence down instead of thirty notes up?"

"Not all my fault, Cliff. You didn't have to put your twenty pence in the cat thing. You could have just jingled your finger in the net like you do at church collection." Ben was staring at

Ariadne's Craft Market. There was a hopeful look on his face.

"What?" said Cliff.

"Ariadne's Craft Market," said Ben slowly.

"So? Ariadne's a witch. They're all witches in there, Slime said so. They're nutty as muesli. They even sell home-made broomsticks."

"Maybe. But they don't have electronic tills," said Ben calmly. Cliff stood up on the fountain wall and looked.

"Don't be obvious," said Ben. "You're supposed to be the professional criminal."

"You're learning fast," said Cliff with reluctant admiration. "O.K. This is the plan," he said, taking control again before Ben got uppity. "We'll go to three of those stall things . . . the basket one, then that healthy herb place with the plants and pillows . . . then the pottery one. She's got her takings in a box on the counter. Silly cow, we'll hit her . . ."

"Hang about . . ."

" 'Hit' as in 'relieve of', you jerk! I'll do it. You create the diversion. We're looking for a present, right? All you've got to do is knock over that leaning tower of plant pots . . . then make a fuss helping her pick them up again. Take your time . . ."

"What if they break and I have to pay for them?"

"Don't let them break. Just sort of scatter them . . ."

"Oh, just scatter them, easy!" Ben said

sarcastically. Then he stiffened. "That girl's watching us. Kathy, the Sally Army girl who got Slime into trouble – she's coming over!"

"Hullo, you two!"

"Us?"

"Yes. Going to Ariadne's? They've got super presents."

"Yes." and "No." said Cliff and Ben together.

"Suit yourselves," said Kathy cheerfully. "I haven't got my Mum a birthday present yet." She glanced from one to the other curiously. Cliff and Ben shuffled their feet.

"I'm glad I've bumped into you," Kathy went on. "You're friends of Simon Hawkins, aren't you?"

"Yes." and "No." Cliff and Ben said together again, like a double comedy act.

"Well, whatever you are . . . will you tell him that Kathy says she's really sorry for what happened, you know, with Ian Carter, the fight? I didn't mean to upset him. I was going to meet him, it was all a misunderstanding . . ."

"We'll tell him," said Cliff. "Now we've got to go, O.K.?"

"Thanks. See you!" Kathy went into Ariadne's Market, Cliff and Ben sighed and waited until she came out with a dead flower arrangement in a vase. She saw them still hovering and frowned to herself as she walked down to Harmony Records.

"O.K., Ben?"

"O.K.," said Ben, trying to convince himself. "O.K."

They were better at it this time. When the Craft people gave their evidence later, they said they had been nice, earnest boys, looking for a present for their teacher who was leaving. One had called his friend Harry and the other Joe . . . maybe they were a bit, well, forced and too jovial? Hard to tell really . . .

They got to the pottery stall, which was the one run by Ariadne herself. "Do you think she'd like one of those plant pots?" Cliff said in a way that suggested he was desperate to find something suitable at last. "How about that one?" He pointed, "The one at the top of the pile? Mind how you go!"

The plant pots teetered obligingly, Ben did a brilliant comedy act trying to catch them. They were plastic, made to look convincingly like earthenware. "Cheats!" he muttered as they bounced hollowly round the Craft Market. Cliff tripped over one and measured his length on the floor. The stallholders gathered round as he picked himself up, rubbing his shoulder and complaining.

"Is he all right?"

"Must be. Better take him to First Aid though."

"Where's that?"

"Upstairs, isn't it? We don't want to be done for negligence or whatever it is . . . Industrial injury?"

"I'm fine," said Cliff, getting to his feet and realizing the plot had failed and it was better to get out and try a new strategy before he and Ben became too familiar. "Better be getting back."

"That's another fine mess you got me into," Cliff said, as they made their way down the Mall.

"You mean a fine mess *I* got *you* out of!" said Ben, nudging him and letting him have a glimpse of the tight roll of notes in his hand.

Cliff's smile changed the shape of his face. "You didn't . . . You did! You did it!" Ben smiled too, proudly. "Well, you created the diversion," he said modestly.

"There must be at least fifty quid there! You're brilliant. Come on. We've got to get out of here fast."

"Is Simon O.K.?"

"Happy as a sandboy. He's got the shed down and now he's building something with the good bits."

"What?" asked Mrs Bates, intrigued.

"That's his secret. But I think it's going to be a tree house. He's borrowed the rope from the garage. He's cleaned out the tool box and mended the garage door as well. I'll be sorry in a way when he goes back to school!"

By mid afternoon Simon had got the platform for the tree house into the cleft of the willow tree. He started to assemble the walls, and realized there weren't enough long nails left. Mr Bates was no handyman, his tool box revealed that. Neither of the Bates were around. He had fifty pence of his pocket money left. He could slip into town and buy some nails and be back in fifteen minutes. Surely there couldn't be any harm in that?

Fangs' Gang were delighted to have found a worthy cause. Nothing quite like it had happened since they'd joined the Animal Rights people demonstrating in a fur shop and spray-painted thousands of pounds' worth of fur coats.

"Poncey load of boutiques in that Mall!" Fangs muttered. "They've had this coming." He hadn't forgiven Papa Grozzi for refusing to serve the gang in his boulevard cafe. A table through his window would make a lovely mess. Some paint for the Indian shop, Bizarre! That'd teach them to call the police when the gang gate-crashed their bhangra parties. Other members had other grievances against the Mall shop-keepers. Like the rat Hodson at Harmony Records who wouldn't sell them adult videos he kept in the back of the shop. They'd get them now all right.

Fangs' spies came back from the Mall and drew a map showing the emergency exits and reported on the security arrangements.

"We need a diversion," said Ivan the Terrible. "I'll smoke-bomb the escalator."

"No!" Fangs glared at him. He was getting to hate Ivan. He was having too many ideas these days. Some of the younger gang members were beginning to look up to him. Fangs was feeling

71

his leadership threatened. He loosened the top set of his teeth with his tongue and moved them around in his mouth dangerously. Ivan didn't flinch.

"No bomb," he said. "Your bombs are unstable. Like yourself. I don't want a lot of people getting into a panic."

"You're getting soft, Fangs."

"Shut your face. I'm the boss. We're going in this afternoon at four. Shut up arguing and listen. This is how it's going to be . . ."

Simon bought his nails and stopped to chat to the owner of the ironmongers'. It was nearly four when he left. He decided to take a short cut through the Mall. Delicious baking smells wafted from Pattie's Pantry and he suddenly felt hungry. Amanda was cleaning the glass shelves.

"Anything for . . . fifteen pence," he asked, counting his change.

"'Fraid not," she smiled regretfully.

"Go on, you must have had some failures that you can sell cheap."

"You want to lose me my job? I've just got it. Hang on, there's a sausage roll that got stuck to the foil. You can have that." She went to get it. There was a sound of breaking glass somewhere in the distance. Cliff and Ben came running along the Mall like frightened rabbits.

"Cliff? Ben? What's wrong?" They skidded to a stop.

"Slime! Gawd, Slime, take this! She'll get us . . ."

They ran on. Simon looked at the wad of notes they had thurst into his hand.

"Here. Your sausage roll. What's that you've got?" said Amanda curiously.

"Nothing," he said, shoving the money deep into his pocket.

"What's that smell?" said Amanda suddenly, wrinkling her nose.

"Smoke," said Simon, tensing. There was another crash of glass and shouting echoed through the Mall. People were looking back fearfully. Simon and Amanda exchanged worried looks. There was danger in the air. "You got a back way out?" Simon asked. She nodded. Simon set off after Ben and Cliff angrily. They'd clearly been up to no good. And now they'd involved him.

"That's all I need," he thought bitterly and tried to stuff the money through the bottom of his jeans' pocket.

Chapter Eight

The panic grew and spread through Monk's Way like a fire. People were screaming with fear and anger. Fangs' Gang seemed to draw excitement from that fear and they became more and more reckless, turning over tables, wrenching seats from their mounts, smashing lights and windows. Shops were ransacked or spray-painted as the mob rushed through shouting obscenely.

Simon forced his way against the crowd trying to get out. He found Cliff and Ben cowering behind a telephone booth. He dragged them out and pointed them towards an emergency exit that only the staff knew about.

He was about to follow them himself when he saw Ivan the Terrible, a wicked grin on his face, pause to throw one of his home-made smoke bombs on to the escalator.

"No! For God's sake!" The escalator was crowded with shoppers and children. It could be disastrous. They had had a talk about fire risks and procedures and how to avoid panic starting in a crowd from Mrs Benson. Not that Simon remembered it precisely at that second. He only knew that he had to move fast to stop Ivan. Pushing people aside he rushed at him. Ivan saw him coming at the last minute, made a desperate lunge to launch his missile and failed. The two boys rolled over each other, the smoke bomb started belching foul-smelling fumes and rolled towards the fountain. Security alarms went off, the sprinkler system started and there was a distant wail of police sirens.

Soon the streets round the Mall were cordoned off and there were firemen running about with hoses and enough police to manage a Cup Final.

Simon was picked up and none too gently slammed into a police van with some of Fangs' Gang. They were separated at the police station and put in different bare rooms waiting to be interviewed. Sergeant Turnbull got Simon. He glanced up as he came in, noted his torn shirt, smoke-blackened face and arms and sighed heavily.

"You again. Might have known it. Turn your pockets out. I don't need to ask your name."

Simon emptied his pockets. There wasn't much in them. A screw of paper with a dozen 3-inch nails and a roll of five pound notes.

"That's nice," sneered the Sergeant, "Oh, that's very nice." He poked the packet of nails with his finger. "Nails," he said unnecessarily, "It's always handy to have a few long nails about you. We'll find out what you were going to do with those in due course." He gave Simon an unpleasant smile, and took the rubber band off the money. "Lot of money for a young lad. Isn't it?"

"It's not mine," muttered Simon helplessly.

"I'm sure it's not yours," Sergeant Turnbull said quietly. He picked up his pen and started to write. Simon stared at a worn patch on the check lino. It couldn't get any worse, could it? Everything had piled up against him. Nothing he could say would help him now. So that was it. He would say nothing. Nothing at all.

"Cliff? You awake?"

"Course I am. How can I sleep?"

"He's not back. It's after eleven. Bates hasn't come back either. Where are they?"

"How do I know?"

"Let's go and ask Mrs Bates."

"No!" Cliff got out of bed and put his dressing-gown on. He sat on Ben's bed in silence for a while. "We've just got to keep quiet. We start asking questions . . . well, then. No one knows we'd been down the stupid shopping place."

76

"Slime does. They'll have found the money, won't they?"

"Must have done. They took him to the police station. Korky saw him. But they can't keep him there. Not at his age. They don't do things like that . . ."

"What then?" said Ben, sounding tearful.

"Don't you start crying or I'll hit you," said Cliff, who was close to crying himself.

"But it's our fault. Everything. I was really scared when I saw that lot breaking everything and shouting and . . . the smoke and . . . but we started it!"

"We didn't know it was going to be that bad though, did we?"

"But it was! People might have been killed. Some must have been hurt, all because we went to Fangs' lot."

"We went to get justice for Slime, that's all. We didn't ask for a full-scale riot, did we? It's just the money. That's what's really bad. Oh gawd, Ben! That's *really* bad."

"I took it. Stole it. You didn't. I'm going to tell Mrs Bates!"

Ben tried to get out of bed and Cliff sat on his head. "Shut up, you stupid creep! Listen! Stop struggling and *listen*! We don't know what Slime's said about the money. Maybe he made up something, got away with it. We could go and blow everything and make things worse. We don't *know* what's happening, so we gotta keep quiet till we do. Right?"

"Yes," said Ben doubtfully. "What if we got some money, put it back where we stole it. Then, well, what Slime's got wouldn't be stolen any more, would it?"

Cliff thought about that one. It made a sort of cockeyed sense. "That's all right *if* we got some money, and *if* we could get it back to the old witch. But I think we've got to keep away from Monk's Way for a long time."

"I wish Slime would come back. It gets worse every minute."

"Kathy? You're not going down to Harmony today, are you?"

"Yes, Mum. Why not?"

"I just don't like the thought of it after yesterday. All that violence in a place like Corbury. What is the world coming to?" She shook her head sadly. "It said on the radio that there were five people taken to hospital. Thousands of pounds' worth of damage. Why? It was started by a school gang. They were just kids! Do you have gangs like that in your school?"

"There are gangs," Kathy said slowly, "but not like that. Bricks have always had a worse record than Banks. I'm glad you didn't send me there." She picked up her bag and grinned reassuringly at her mother.

"It'll be all right today. Don't worry. The place'll be swarming with cops. Anyway, I'll have to go today. They'll need help clearing up."

She met Amanda at the entrance to Monk's Way.

"Phew!" said Amanda. "Seen the mess? It's like a battlefield in there. Poor Grozzis. They had their big window broken. There's glass everywhere."

"I thought you worked at Pattie's now."

"I do – but there's hardly any business going on today so I went to help the Grozzis clear up instead. And Bizarre! poor souls. You know those lovely gold-embroidered saris? Ruined with paint. Apparently that wretch Simon Hawkins was behind it."

"Simon?" said Kathy, concerned. "He couldn't . . . surely . . ."

"He's a vicious type. Look at the fights he's been in."

"Simon's a loner," said Kathy, shaking her head. "He wouldn't have anything to do with a gang."

"Well, they've carted him off to prison or somewhere. He had a load of stolen cash on him when they picked him up, and he and another boy were trying to smoke-bomb the escalator."

"I don't believe it. Anyway, he's only thirteen. He can't be in prison . . ."

At Harmony Records she found Mr Hodson and Paula-Jo stocktaking. The shop seemed undamaged.

"There you are, Kathy," Mr Hodson said as if she were late. He had a habit of making other people think they were always in the wrong.

"Finish this with Paula. I've got to see Mrs Benson about the insurance claim. Get on with it. Don't just stand there."

Paula-Jo grinned at Kathy when he'd gone and went and put on a reggae tape.

"What happened here?" asked Kathy, anxiously.

"We were lucky, I suppose. We just got the tail end of it all. But, wow! Kathy, it was scarey. Like Notting Hill Carnival! They were wild, but crazy wild. There was smoke and screaming . . . glass breaking, and people looting – not just the school gang, I remember some of them. Other people, respectable, you know, just started lifting things when all the pandemonium started. Ariadne lost all her takings before it even got going. We'd better get on with this stocktake. There's a whole lot of tapes and CDs gone walkies."

Every shop had its own story to tell about the trouble. Kathy listened quietly and stored the facts away. She was concerned for Simon. The dreadful vandalism had been started at the two places he claimed had discriminated against him. That would come out. He had certainly harboured grudges. She couldn't believe he would steal. But what about Cliff and Ben? Why had they been hovering outside Ariadne's when she saw them?

Cliff and Ben had a bad day at school worrying about Simon. The only good thing was that

Fangs, and several senior members of his gang who had managed to keep out of the trouble, were having a day off, and the rest of the gang had been suspended.

The headmaster gave the whole school a hard lecture. He told them how saddened he was that his school should have been involved in such a violent episode and asked anyone with information to come forward.

There were several policemen going round the school. Ben and Cliff rendezvoused in the toilets.

"What do you think?"

"About what?"

"Going to the head. Nailing Fangs."

"You're crazy! He'll be back. He'll kill us. Anyway, everyone will know we started it all. Then there's the money . . ."

"I suppose you're right. Maybe Slime'll be back when we get home. Then we can sort it all out."

They hurried back to the The Grange after school. No Simon. Mrs Bates was packing his things in his room.

"Mrs Bates? What . . . where . . . ?"

She pushed a pair of socks into a corner of a hold-all. "Would one of you get Simon's anorak and shoes from the locker room, please?"

"Yes . . . but . . ."

"He's gone to Gresham Lodge for a little while," she smiled at them tiredly. "I hope he'll be back soon. Mr Bates wants to see you both."

Ben and Cliff stood staring at her for a

moment and then they scuttled off to find Simon's things.

"What's Gresham Lodge?" whispered Ben urgently.

"It's a Special Home," said Cliff grimly. "It's for hard cases and nutters. Gordon Smith went there for setting fire to things. Sounds like bad news for Slime. Listen, we don't know anything. Nothing at all. Bates is going to grille us. We've got to be really careful. We never went anywhere near Monk's Way yesterday, right?"

Geoff Bates was standing by the fireplace, scraping his smelly pipe thoughtfully. He glanced at Ben and Cliff's scared faces peering round the door.

"Come in. Sit down, lads. Sit down. I'm not going to eat you. I want to know if you can help your friend Simon."

"Help him, Mr Bates?" said Cliff, "How?"

"Well. You must know he's in a lot of trouble. He seems to have been involved with this gang who broke up the Shopping Mall yesterday. And he had money from the craft market on him. Stolen money." Cliff and Ben did their best to look surprised. Geoff Bates lit his pipe slowly. "Tell me one thing," he said, puffing clouds of smoke. "Were either of you in the Mall yesterday?"

"No," said Cliff firmly.

"Good. I'm very glad to hear it," said Bates, sounding relieved. "Simon didn't steal the money." He paused and puffed again. Ben stole a look at Cliff. "Two younger boys did. It seems to be the pattern with this wretched gang at your school. They terrorise the younger children to get them to steal for them. Have either of you been threatened by this gang? Asked for money, anything like that?"

"No," said Cliff.

"You Ben?"

"No. We keep out of their way."

"Good. Do you know how Simon got mixed up with this gang? It seems most unlike him."

"We didn't know he was, did we Ben?" said Cliff honestly. "He never said anything to us. What's going to happen to him, Mr Bates?"

"He's gone to stay at Gresham Lodge until he comes before the Juvenile Court. They have to make reports about him. The social worker, psychiatrist . . . it's a long story. Obviously I shall do everything I can to help him. Unfortunately he refuses to help himself."

"How's that?"

"He won't say anything in his own defence. Nothing at all. That's why I hoped you could come up with something." He paused and waited expectantly. Ben and Cliff just shook their heads in unison. Geoff Bates looked from one to the other questioningly. "Did Simon come to school yesterday and meet up with the gang?"

"No. He was here, wasn't he?"

"That's what I thought," said Geoff Bates

grimly. "Well, off you go and think about it. The police and the school want to get this gang broken up. You don't have to worry about any repercussions. Anything you tell me will be in confidence. I'd like to think Simon's involvement was one big misunderstanding – that maybe he'd been seriously threatened. I can't believe he'd steal for any other reason. Can you?"

Chapter Nine

"Karen? Hurry up out of there. I've *got* to go to the toilet!"

"Oh, come on in then," said Karen impatiently. Her hair was going all wrong this morning, when she particularly wanted it to look nice. She let Brian, one of the big twins, in and turned back to the mirror. He sat on the lavatory with his Arsenal pyjamas around his ankles watching her.

"You've been putting that muck on your face again."

"Oh, shut up! It's not muck."

"Where you going? Down the Monk's Way Mall again?"

"I don't know what you're talking about. I'm going to the youth club."

"Barry's friend said he saw you. In a shop. Like you worked there."

"Well, he got it wrong," said Karen sharply. It wasn't going to last much longer, keeping her job a secret from the family. She'd known it wouldn't. Soon they'd all know and they'd be borrowing money from her as if she were a building society.

"Mickey Evans' sister's got shoes made out of a snake," observed Brian, considering it carefully.

"Yes?" Shoes were a safer topic.

"He says she slithers about in them like this," he said, weaving his hands about sinuously.

"Eergh! Phew! What a pong!"

"I can't help it. It's the cabbage. Mum shouldn't make me eat it. Anyway, you're not going down the youth club or anywhere today."

"Who says?' said Karen quickly.

"Everyone says. You got to stay and look after Danny. We're all going out in Mr Jordan's van."

"It's Saturday. You'll be going to the jumble."

"We're going in the van. I told you. You're babysitting again!" he said jubilantly.

"We'll see about that!" said Karen, giving up on her hair and stalking out.

"I don't know what you're fussing about, Karen," said her mother, "You don't have to stay in all day. Take him down to the youth club with you. I've made up his bottles and things."

"We're rehearsing this play . . ."

"You said you were playing badminton. He can watch."

"What if he cries? Oh, Mum! No one else takes babies. Anyway he's not dressed and I'm late . . ."

"It's all right, Danny," she said to the gurgling baby as she pushed the battered pram into the town. "I'm not cross with you. But I've got to go to work and I don't know what Mrs Kendall will say."

The pram lurched on its wonky wheel and Danny laughed so much that she had to do it again. They went along in a series of giggles and bumps and nearly sent Jake flying.

"Hi, Karen! What have you got there?"

"A baby, you dumb cluck! What does it look like."

"And you so young!" Jake said teasingly. "What's her name?"

"Danny. Can't you tell boys from girls?"

"Course. Just joking. You can tell he's a boy – he's got that butch, superior sort of look. He's sweet. What are you going to do, take him to work?"

"I'm lumbered for the day." She gave Jake a hopeful little smile. "You like babies?"

"Yes. I do. I've got this little sister . . . I often look after her."

"A baby in a toy shop would be O.K., wouldn't it?"

"What do you mean?"

"Jake, be a real friend. Take Danny to the toy

shop while I talk Mrs Kendall round, will you? It's important. I've got something special to do today. Look, you can tell he likes you. He never smiles at strangers like that normally."

"Doesn't he?" said Jake, pleased. "Hey, Danny, you want to come to work with Uncle Jake? You do? Has he got a bottle or something?"

"Oh, yes. He's fully equipped. Thanks, Jake. He'll go to sleep soon, he's ever so good. I'll come and get him as soon as I can." She took a parcel out of the pram and ran off with a wave.

"Good grief!" said Esther Chandler, looking through the toy shop window, "Jake's coming. He's pushing a pram! Surely he's not bringing his sister . . ."

"It's just a little baby," said Daph, joining her. "The sister's four, isn't she? Well, he looks happier today, thank goodness."

"Don't be unkind. Poor kid doesn't have much to make him happy these days."

"Morning!" said Jake brightly as he manoeuvred the pram into the shop and tucked Danny up professionally.

"Morning, Jake. What's this?"

"This is Danny. Isn't he sweet? Can he stay here for a little while? I thought you wouldn't mind . . . his Mum's having her hair done," he said quickly. "He won't be any trouble."

"Bless him. Look at his little fingers," said Daph, drooling over the pram. Esther grunted.

She looked at the battered pram and thought it didn't quite go with a woman who was having her hair done in Monk's Way.

"He'd better be quiet," she said. "Now then, Jake, you can get on with filling up the boxed cars. Then keep an eye on the pocket money stall, it being Saturday. We've been losing a lot of stuff recently."

"What, shoplifting?" asked Jake. Esther and Daph looked at each other and Daph shook her head warningly. Jake was suddenly very busy in the stock room.

Mrs Kendall was just taking down the grille when Karen arrived at Victoriana. "You're early, dear," she said.

"Yes. I wondered if I could take a bit of time off during the morning. I'll work later if you like."

"I should think that'll be O.K. We're not going to be rushed off our feet. Business has been dreadful since all that wrecking stuff happened. Not that I blame people for staying away – but security's so tight I had trouble getting in myself this morning. Flick a duster over the window, will you, please? Got shopping to do, have you?"

"Yes . . . a couple of things. You know Binney Braden, the children's author?"

"Binney . . . Yes, she writes The Busybodies, doesn't she? My niece watches them on the telly. She's got a dinky little T-shirt with them on. Bit young for you though."

"Oh yes. My little brothers watch Busybodies. She came to our school and was ever so nice. She did a workshop encouraging us to write stories. I carried her bag to the car afterwards and she said if I ever wrote anything she'd look at it."

"And have you? Written something?" She picked up Karen's parcel from the counter, "Is this it? Can I have a look?"

"Well . . ."

"Oh, go on! You're going to show Binney Thinggy so you can't be shy!" Karen blushed and concentrated on her dusting while Mrs Kendall leafed through the exercise book. She started to chuckle gently and then she laughed out loud. "Oh, Karen, this is hilarious! Wherever did you get the idea?"

"Oh, The Troofs . . . it's just something I made up for my brothers."

"Did you do the drawings as well?"

"Yes. They're just rough. I know someone who's got a sister who might do them professionally . . ."

"Don't! These are charming. I love the way the little Troof goes Boing! when he's surprised. You are a clever girl!"

"Thanks," said Karen, pleased, and wondering if this was the time to mention the matter of Danny abandoned in the toy shop.

"You're cleverer than you know," Mrs Kendall went on as she unlocked the till and put her float in the drawer. She turned to Karen with a handful of crisp new five-pound notes fanned out like a card hand.

"What's that for?" asked Karen, puzzled.

"Take it. It's yours. That load of junk you bought at the jumble sale – most of it was utter tat, but the beads you described as squashed sweeties were amber and I sold them yesterday."

"But . . . but there's fifty pounds here!"

"Amber's very collectable. Don't worry, I've taken my percentage."

Karen took the money and started to laugh. "I wasn't going to buy the squashed sweets! I chose all the tat – one of the little twins grabbed them!"

"Well, you'd better buy him a big lolly," said Mrs Kendall. "Put the kettle on, there's a love, and we'll have a cuppa. Put that money in a safe place. An awful lot of things are being nicked around here."

Danny was as good as Karen said he would be. He slept peacefully in his pram for more than an hour and would have done so longer, but a harassed mother with a troupe of little children came into the toy shop. The smallest started jiggling the pram.

"Leave it alone," said Jake.

"Baby, baby!" said the child, jiggling more fiercely.

"Yes, baby," said Jake. "Now push off. Baby's sleeping, O.K.?"

"Baby wake up, baby cry!" said the child evilly. "Make baby cry."

"I'll make you cry in a minute!" hissed Jake. The child suddenly stopped rocking the pram, seized Danny's arm and bit it. Danny let out an enraged shriek.

"There!" said the child triumphantly. "Baby cry!" Jake rushed to comfort Danny and pushed the obnoxious child away roughly. The child started to bawl at the top of its voice.

"Jake!" said Esther firmly. "It's time that baby was returned to its mother. Hurry along, we need you here."

"O.K., I'll take him now," said Jake, slipping the pram brake and pushing the crying Danny away. He couldn't see Karen in Victoriana. Mrs Kendall was busy with a customer. Danny had gone quiet, Jake was trying to park him just inside the door, then he realized Danny was only quiet because he was gathering breath for a new wave of bellowing. Jake tried to signal to Mrs Kendall that he was leaving Danny for Karen. She signalled back furiously to him to take him away. He turned the pram and scuttled back down the Mall, rummaging in the pram with one hand. He found a bottle of milk and another of juice just as he was going by the Grozzis' restaurant.

"O.K., Danny. Coffee break." He sat down at one of the outer tables where Danny could see the fountains. He fitted the teat on the bottle, screwed it up and put it on the table. Papa Grozzi looked with horror as he lifted Danny out and plugged him into the bottle.

"What you do?" he said. "You think this is a nursery?"

"Sorry. Baby's hungry," said Jake apologetically. Papa Grozzi gazed at the shabby pram. "What you going to order then?"

"I'm afraid I can't order anything. I haven't any money. All right, I'll go." Danny started to yell again when Jake took the bottle away.

"Good grief, Jake! What are you doing with that baby?" asked Kathy Roberts, sitting down at the table. "Hullo, Papa. Coffee and a doughnut, please." Papa smiled and nodded.

"Thank goodness you're here!" Jake said, setting up Danny's bottle again. "Can you give him this? I've got to get back to work and he's thirsty."

"But . . . but . . ." Kathy protested as he thrust Danny at her and she picked up the bottle. Danny sucked it noisily and looked up at her trustingly with big tear-laden eyes. Kathy looked at him lovingly.

"Hey, Jake! Come back! Whose baby is it? What am I supposed to do with him?"

"He's Danny," Jake called as he retreated, "Take him to Karen at Victoriana when he's finished." Kathy played with Danny as she had her coffee. Even Papa Grozzi came round and made chooky-chooky noises at him.

Mrs Kendall didn't come round. "Take that scrubby pram away. Someone else tried to dump it in here," she hissed.

"But Karen . . ."

"Karen's gone out. Sorry, Mr Gribble," she said, turning back to her customer . . .

Kathy pushed Danny down to Harmony Records, and parked the pram in the video section where Danny could see the coloured lights.

"You're late back, Kathy," said Mr Hodson. "I'm going to put a stop to these coffee breaks. Get into the stock room and find these quickly," he said, handing her a piece of paper. "What's that pram doing there?"

"Er . . . I said I'd look after it for a customer, just for a little while," said Kathy quickly.

"This isn't a ruddy crèche! Paula-Jo, keep an eye on this pram!" Paula-Jo came over and peered into the pram.

"It's got a baby in it!" she said in surprise.

"God! I'm surrounded by idiots. Kathy, get that stock!"

Kathy scuttled into the stock room where Ian Carter was unpacking cassettes. "Ian, help me!"

"Why? What's wrong?"

"There's a baby in a pram in the videos."

"A what?"

"Baby. Can you take it back to Jake? It's really Karen's but she's not there. It's your coffee break. Please . . ."

"Kathy!" Mr Hodson was standing in the door looking furious.

"I'm coming, Mr Hodson," she said, flustered. Ian crept out and found Danny gurgling at a poster for a horror video. He had never pushed a

94

pram before. He couldn't take the brake off. The pram skittered and jerked across the tiled pavement.

"Ian! What are you doing with that pram?"

"Taking the baby to the toy shop," said Ian, blushing. Mrs Benson looked into the pram. "Poor little mite's getting a bit bashed about. Why don't you take the brake off?" She did it for him and looked at him curiously. "Sweet baby. Boy or girl?"

"Er . . . girl," guessed Ian.

"What's her name?"

"Kathy," said Ian promptly.

"Something to do with the Chandlers?" Mrs Benson queried.

"Yes, that's right. Better be going."

Mrs Benson watched him go with a smile. Really, she thought, these kids have to do everything here!

Chapter Ten

Ian walked self-consciously down Monk's Way behind Danny's pram. The baby was making loud squeaky noises and Ian wished she'd just go quietly to sleep. He hovered outside the toy shop. There was no sign of Jake.

"Excuse me . . ." he said from the door. Daph looked up from some parcels with a piece of string in her mouth.

"Danny's back," she mumbled, "with a new driver!" Annie, thought Ian. So that's her name.

"I'm looking for Jake. He's to take Annie."

"Now, look here!" said Esther, coming up behind him. "It's time that baby went back to its mother."

"Fine," said Ian. "Where is she?"

"Having her hair done apparently," said

Esther rather impatiently. "It's not fair to expect you kids to babysit when you've got jobs to do. She must be at the new salon. It's just opened, you know? Herbs?"

"O.K. I'll take her there now," said Ian, and managed a three-point-turn with the pram.

"Did he say 'her'?" said Daph, confused. "When Jake brought that baby in it was a boy! I suppose it's all right. Maybe we should tell Mrs Benson . . . What if the poor love's been abandoned?"

Ian found a sign pointing up a staircase to Herbs Hairstyles. The other Herbs shops had still not been opened. He took a few steps back and looked up at the windows. He could see women sitting under driers or having things done to them by girls in pink overalls. A hot perfumed smell wafted down the stairs. He couldn't possibly go up there. He felt hot and bothered. He'd be in trouble with Hodson soon. He couldn't go back with Annie . . .

"Ian, what *are* you doing?" Amanda gave a shriek of laughter. "Who's this in the pram?"

"It's Annie," said Ian miserably.

"Hullo, Annie!" Amanda bent over the pram. "Whew! Time she had her nappy changed, isn't it?"

"Don't say things like that!"

"Sorry. Well, what are you doing? Taking her to have a perm?"

"It's not funny. Jake was looking after her and he dumped her on Kathy, and she asked me to take her to the toyshop and they said her mother was having her hair done and I just can't go up there . . ." Ian stopped and looked at her helplessly.

"That's no problem," said Amanda brightly. "I'll take her. I want to have a look round up there." She looked at the rather stained baby in its battered pram and thought it was going to look a bit out of place in a smart new hairdressers'.

"Oh, thanks. Thanks a million, Mandy!" said Ian, backing away.

"O.K.," said Amanda. "What's the mother called?"

"It's Karen's mother . . ."

"Karen's? You sure?"

When Karen slipped out to go to the bookshop she had checked on Danny, and found him sleeping peacefully in the toy shop. Good old Jake, she thought. I'll pick Danny up later and buy something nice for Jake.

There was a big crowd in the bookshop to see Binney Braden. Karen bought three of her books for the boys with her jumble wealth and got in the queue to get them signed.

"It's one for Barry and Brian, one for Keith and Lenny and one for Jimmy and little Danny, please," she said. Binney Braden smiled and started on the first one.

"Miss Braden," Karen said hesitantly . . . "You came to our school last term . . ."

"Did I, dear? Where was that?"

"Redland comprehensive . . . and you said if I finished a book you'd look at it . . ."

"Well, of course . . ." Binney Braden signalled to her editor who came and took Karen over. "It's always useful meeting a publisher," she said to her with a wink. "This is Barbara Chigwell from Playtime Publications."

"Come over here," said Barbara Chigwell, taking Karen's parcel from her. "I expect Binney told you it's quite difficult for new authors to find someone to publish their first book?"

"Oh, yes," said Karen, apologetically. "It's good of you to bother. These are just some stories I made up for my little brothers. I suppose lots of sisters do that?"

"They do indeed," said Barbara Chigwell with a wry smile. She flicked through the pages. "Your drawings? They're nice and simple." She was quiet for a few minutes.

"How old are you Karen?"

"Thirteen and a half."

"Really? Well, you've got an original idea here. Of course . . . it's not quite book-shaped as it stands . . . but . . . I like the laid-back granny, she's terrific . . . the dialogue's nice and crisp . . . can you wait a few minutes?"

Karen waited, getting increasingly uneasy about Danny and Mrs Kendall. Finally Barbara Chigwell came back and said she would like to take the book back to London and show it to someone else. Karen wrote down her address with shaking fingers. She had never expected anything so important to happen to her Troofs as to be taken back to London by a real publisher . . .

She rushed out of the book shop and tore down the Mall to the toy shop. There was no sign of Danny, his pram or Jake. The two Chandler sisters were busy with customers.

"Sorry to interrupt," said Karen urgently. "There was a baby . . ."

Esther Chandler excused herself from her customer. "Look, I don't know what's going on," she said, "but Jake brought a baby in earlier called Danny . . ."

"Yes, that's him . . ."

"Then he took it away again somewhere, and then another boy, that shy one from the record shop, brought it back and said it was a girl and then he took it to the hairdressers'. O.K.?"

"No! What hairdressers'? Why?" Esther shrugged.

"The one where its mother is, I suppose. You kids seem to be playing hide-and-seek with the poor little thing."

Karen was in a panic now. She rushed up to Victoriana. "Mrs Kendall, did someone bring a baby . . ."

"Ssh, Karen. I'm busy," hissed Mrs Kendall. "A couple of your friends have been trying to dump a dreadful old pram here . . ."

"Where is it now?"

"God knows! . . . Karen, come back . . ."

"I can't. I've got to find Danny!" She rushed

off again almost in tears and bumped into Jake outside the Grozzis'.

"Jake! Where is he? Where's Danny?"

"Kathy took him back to Victoriana . . . didn't she?"

"No! He's not there. He's not anywhere. He's been kidnapped. He must have been! No, wait! Your boss said something about a hairdresser. There isn't one here . . . is there?"

"Calm down," said Jake, who was beginning to panic himself. "Here's Mama Grozzi. Mama! Is there a hairdresser here?"

"Si, Mr 'erbs just open today. Something wrong with you's two?"

"Have you seen a baby . . ."

"Ah! That baby. So sad. How anyone could do that to so little a baby I don't know. The police came and took it away."

Karen went so white she was almost transparent. Her legs buckled and she collapsed at a table and burst into tears.

Danny was getting used to the changing faces of his minders. He glugged and gurgled happily to Amanda in the lift going up to Herbs Hairstyles. "You're a pretty girl," said Amanda, tidying up the pram. "Funny, Karen didn't say she had a sister. I thought it was all brothers."

The Herbs receptionist was sitting at a high desk answering telephones. She didn't see the pram at first.

"Hullo," she said wearily. "You come about the job?"

"Job?" said Amanda, instantly alert. "What sort of job?"

"Gopher. Make the coffees, sweep up, do a bit of washing, taking rollers out, you know. We were expecting someone about your age, but she hasn't turned up."

"Can I have an interview then?" said Amanda eagerly. She liked the idea of working in a hair salon. It would be a hundred times nicer than Pattie's Pantry.

"I don't know. I'll have to go and ask." She was gone a long time, the phones kept ringing and she came back flustered.

"Sorry, they're all at sixes and sevens . . . the head stylist's thrown a wobbly and everyone's going round on tiptoe. Come back later, O.K.?" She answered two phones at once. Amanda gestured to the pram and mouthed "Baby . . ." The receptionist was getting an earful on the phone. She gave Amanda her look of sorely tried patience and pushed a pad and pencil across.

Amanda wrote THE BABY'S ANNIE GREEN. MOTHER HAVING HAIR DONE. SEE YOU LATER, then she blew 'Annie' a kiss and left.

Danny dozed for a little and then he woke up hungry and said so, loudly. The receptionist dropped the phones, stared at the pram in horror and read Amanda's note.

"What the hell's going on in here?" said the manageress, boiling in like an enraged turkey. "What's that baby doing?"

"A girl brought it . . ." the receptionist said weakly. "I've been busy . . . there's a note saying she belongs to a Mrs Green who's having her hair done . . ."

The manageress glowered. "That baby doesn't belong to one of our customers," she said slowly, "there's no one called Green . . . What sort of a girl left it?"

"She was about fourteen, nicely spoken . . . You don't think . . . oh, no!"

The manageress picked Danny up and he looked expectantly for his bottle. "Bring the pram into the toilet," she snapped. "Now have a good look. Is there a note?"

"No." The receptionist lifted the mattress. "There's a bottle, some clothes . . ."

"Give me the bottle and go and ring the police at once!"

Danny settled into his new surroundings at the police station. He'd been changed and fed and the policewoman looking after him now was a lot calmer than the other people had been. The policewoman was thinking of a temporary name for him while his details were being fed into the police computer.

Another policewoman came in and her face lit up. "What's Danny Green doing here?" she said in surprise.

The police car drove up to the Green's house at the same time as the family came back in the Jordans' van. "Blimey, it's the law!" said Mr Green. "Drive round the block again." Mr Jordan nodded grimly. There were boxes of radios and cassette players in the back that had been bought very cheaply, no questions asked.

"Wait!" said Mrs Green suddenly. "That policewoman, she's called Rosemary . . ."

"You got friends in high places?" said Mr Jordan suspiciously.

"She came round when we had that bother with the big twins. She stopped at home with Danny while I went down to the station. Maybe there's something wrong . . . something's happened to Karen and Danny. Go back!"

She jumped out of the car and ran anxiously to the policewoman. Her face changed colour, her mouth dropped open and she hurried back to the van.

"It's Danny. They've taken him down the police station!"

"They've what? They can't. They can't arrest a baby, even one of ours!"

Jake put his arm round Karen's trembling shoulders. "Come on," he said, "we'll go to Mrs Benson. She'll know what to do. I'm sorry, Karen, it was my fault. I *was* looking after Danny. He's a terrific little baby, and he's *all right*!"

"He must have been frightened . . ."

104

"He's too little . . ."

"My Mum and Dad'll kill me . . ."

"Bet they don't. Come on Karen. You're a big close family. They'll understand. I'll tell them it was all my fault." He gave her shoulders a friendly squeeze.

"Thanks, Jake. You really are . . ."

"O.K. Don't start crying again. Here, have my handkerchief . . ." He held out a limp, dirty bit of rag. She took it and held it, her red eyes latched on to his and held his gaze. Jake wanted to hug her for a very long time. "Come on," he said instead. "There seems to be a protest meeting going on in Mrs Benson's office."

News about the abandoned baby had spread like wildfire around the shopping centre. A very young policeman was poking about in Danny's deserted pram. Amanda was protesting she had been handed a baby girl, as if it had been a game of liar dice. The policeman's radio squawked. "The parents are at the police station now. They've identified the child as Danny Green," he told Mrs Benson.

Mrs Benson looked up and saw Karen and Jake. "You two!" she said, shaking her head. "Look what you started!"

"I'm sorry . . ." said Karen in a tiny, shaking voice.

"I bet you are," said Mrs Benson kindly. "Come along, I'll drive you down to the police station."

"Thanks, Mrs Benson," Karen sniffed.

"Shall I come with you?" asked Jake.

"Would you?" She looked at him gratefully.

"Course." He took her hand. "It'll be all right. You'll see. Can I have my hanky back now?"

Find out what happens to the kids at the Mall in Book 4: Money Matters.